by

Douglas Hill

LONDON
VICTOR GOLLANCZ LTD
1986

First published in Great Britain August 1979
by Victor Gollancz Ltd,
14 Henrietta Street, London WC2E 8QJ
Second impression March 1981
Third impression May 1982
Fourth impression November 1983
Fifth impression October 1986

ISBN 0-575-02663-4

Printed in Great Britain by
St Edmundsbury Press Ltd, Bury St Edmunds, Suffolk

For my son
Michael

part one
Death of a world

chapter one

He had been walking the dirty streets since twilight first began
to gather. The pain streamed like liquid fire through every cell
of his body – but he locked it away in a corner of his mind,
ignored it, and walked.

There was little to please the eye in his surroundings, and he
paid scant attention to them. He was on a small poor unimportant planet whose very name, Coranex, meant nothing to
him. But around the spaceport clustered a drab, seedy town,
which was a well-known stopover on the main space lanes. It
attracted freightermen, traders, wandering technicians, space
drifters of every sort. Those were the people he was looking
for. Those were the people most likely to pick up the kind of
information he desperately sought.

He threaded his way through the clatter and glitter of the
streets, thronged with people idling past the tawdry attractions
offered to space-weary visitors – everything from ordinary
holoscreens to shadowy, semi-illicit drug dives. Methodically
he worked his way from place to place, concentrating mainly
on the attendants, doorkeepers, bartenders – those in a position to collect and distil the talk, the gossip, of their hundreds
of customers.

But he also watched faces in the crowds. Many people turned towards him with a flicker of curiosity – their interest caught
for a moment by his tall leanness, the controlled litheness of
his movements, most of all by the grey-black uniform with the
brilliant, sky-blue circlet on shoulder and upper chest. Sometimes a person would glance at him curiously and then look
again, with a flicker of recognition in their eyes. And then the

uniformed man would pause, and intercept, and ask his questions.

Always the answers were the same. A shrug, a shake of the head, a negative. Sometimes a shadow of sympathy – most often the blankness of indifference. The Inhabited Galaxy was a big place; everybody had problems of their own.

Undeterred, he kept moving, as he had on a dozen planets or more before Coranex – while the pain clamoured for his full attention, while twilight darkened into deep night. His head remained high and his shoulders square, for a lifetime of military training cannot be erased in a few months – not by pain, not by weariness, not by loneliness, not even by despair.

Despair was near enough, though, ready to overwhelm him. He knew how much time he had left to go on searching. It was a good deal less than the time he had already spent. Yet in those months he had picked up nothing except scattered hints, all of them vague, fragmentary. They were enough to keep him going – but they were never enough to give his search some point, some clear direction.

But he kept on. He had nothing else to do. And the fiery pain in his body was nothing compared to the grim, vengeful determination that fuelled his search.

He was Keill Randor, once the youngest and, some said, the finest Strike Group Leader in the 41st Legion of the planet Moros.

But now he was a soldier without an army, a wanderer without a home, a man without a people.

And he was dying.

The bar was dim, half-empty, squalid, stinking of stale spilled drink and unwashed bodies. The bartender was an off-worlder, from one of the 'altered worlds' – where, over the centuries, local conditions had caused changes, mutations, in the humans who inhabited them. He was dwarfish and stocky, orange-skinned and hairless. But his shrug, when Keill asked his question, was an exact replica of all the others Keill had met in his searching.

'Legionaries? I heard what happened to 'em. Nothin' else. Anyway, got no time to stand around jawin', pickin' up rumours. Got a business t' run.'

The orange-skinned dwarf moved as if to turn away, but glanced up at Keill and changed his mind. Keill's expression had not altered, but something in his eyes told the bartender that, if he moved, he might not enjoy what would happen next.

Keill took out a handful of the plastic wafers that were galactic credits, selected one, and laid it on the bar. 'Is there anyone,' he said evenly, 'who might have had time to listen to rumours?'

The bartender's hand covered the credit, and pondered for a long moment. 'Maybe,' he said at last. 'Freighter pilot named Crask, gets around a lot, has big ears and a big mouth. Might know somethin'.'

'Where do I find him?'

The orange dwarf sneered. 'Blind drunk in an alley somewhere. Unless he's got back to the port. That's where he sleeps – in his ship.'

Keill nodded and left the bar. He did not seem to see the bartender gesture quickly towards a group of heavy-set men slouching over drinks at a nearby table.

A yawning security guard pointed out the freighter owned by the man called Crask. It was a battered hulk of a ship, bulbous and ungainly like all freighters – and it was deserted. Keill settled down to wait. He did not allow himself to hope; he did not allow himself to think about the possibility that Crask might know something, or the stronger possibility that he might be just another dead end. He merely leaned against the ship – relaxed, controlled, infinitely patient – and waited.

The men came soon, as he had half-expected. Four bulky shadows in the dim lighting, which focused mainly on the low buildings across the spaceport's flat plasticrete surface.

They ranged themselves in front of Keill, looking him up and down slowly. Keill had taken in the details of the four in a glance. All of a type – heavy muscle running to fat, soiled one-piece coveralls, hard, empty eyes. Small-time space drifters, who would be more willing to operate on the criminal fringe of interworld trade than off it.

The biggest of the four, almost bald, stood slightly to the front of the others, as if to underline the fact that he was their leader. Keill straightened up slowly, away from the ship, still relaxed and calm.

'I'm Crask,' said the balding man. 'You the one lookin' to hear about legionaries?'

Keill nodded.

'An' you're a legionary yourself?'

'I am.'

'Yeah. Too bad about your planet.'

The words were spoken as if Crask were sympathizing over some minor affliction, like a head-cold.

Keill's expression did not change. 'I was told that you might be able to give me some information.'

'I might,' Crask said. 'What'd it be worth?'

'It depends on what you tell me.'

The big man snorted. 'You want me to tell you what I know – and *then* you name your price?'

'You won't be cheated,' Keill replied.

'Ain't that easy,' Crask said stubbornly. 'Name us some kind o' figure.'

Keill sighed. 'I've got about three thousand galacs. I can pay your price.' He recalled for an instant the day that he had ripped out of his one-man fighter every expendable item he could – second space suit, escape capsule, some of his hand weapons, spare parts – and sold them to help finance his search.

Crask licked his lips. 'You got that kind of money with you?'

'Not here. In my ship.' Keill pointed out into the darkness

of the spaceport, towards the central pad where his ship waited, just as he had left it after landing.

Crask's grin was unpleasant. 'Then let's us walk out there just now, an' you can get y'r money.'

Keill shook his head. 'We'll stay here, you'll tell me what you know, then I'll go and get the money.'

Crask's laughter was even more unpleasant. 'You don't get the idea at all. You're a drifter, a nothin'. You don't know nobody here, nobody knows you. So nobody's gonna raise trouble if you're found face-down in a gutter. Happens all the time t' drifters. Get drugged up, get into trouble, get dead. Nobody cares.'

As he spoke, Crask slid a meaty hand into a pocket and dragged out a slim plastic cylinder. A needle-gun – more likely, Keill knew, to be armed with a killer poison than an anaesthetic.

The other three men also drew out weapons. Two had the knobbly metal clubs favoured by backstreet thugs on many worlds. The third, unusually, had a glowing therm-knife, its blade superheated so that it burned, rather than cut, through most materials – including human flesh.

Keill stood calmly, watching, seeming not to move. Yet his body was gathering itself, balanced, ready.

It was almost unfair.

The thugs were grinning. They saw themselves as four tough, well-armed men facing only one man, empty-handed, helpless.

But they were facing a legionary of Moros. A man whose people were trained – all of them, and from infancy – to the highest pitch in the arts and skills of battle. And a man who, in his own right, had been a leading medal-winner for each of the previous two years in his planet's annual Festival of Martial Games. Many of those medals had been for unarmed combat.

So Crask was still in the process of raising the needler when Keill moved.

13

He gave no hint or warning, did not tense or poise his body. He simply dropped, full-length, to one side.

His right hand met the plasticrete, the arm rigid to take his weight. On the pivot of that hand, his body swung in a horizontal arc, legs scything.

One boot swept the feet out from under a club-wielder. The point of the other boot struck precisely against the beefy wrist of the hand that held the needler.

The crack of bone breaking was nearly drowned by Crask's shriek of pain. As the needle-gun sailed away into darkness, Keill had already flexed his body like a spring and come to his feet.

Crask had staggered and half-fallen, clutching his shattered wrist and moaning. The club-wielder whom Keill had felled was struggling to his feet; the second one had just begun to bring up his club. Keill moved again with the same bewildering speed, slipping under the raised weapon. A rib crunched as Keill's elbow slammed into the thick chest, and the man screamed and collapsed. In the same motion Keill lashed out with his left foot, the blow perfectly timed, burying the point of his toe in the first club-wielder's bulging paunch, sending him hurtling back to collide with the knife-man, both sprawling.

The knife-man picked himself up, staring wide-eyed at Keill, who stood quietly, waiting. Then the therm-blade drew a glowing curve in the air as the man's hand swept back, and threw.

As the white-hot knife spun towards him Keill seemed to sway aside almost lazily. But the other man's eye was not quick enough to follow the movement of the legionary's hand as it flashed up and plucked the knife from the air by its insulated handle.

In a continuation of the same blurred movement, Keill pressed the stud that deactivated the blade, and with a snap of wrist and forearm hurled the knife back.

He had thrown to deliver the knife hilt-first, for he had no wish to kill. The heavy handle made a dull smack as it struck the knife's owner exactly between the eyes. He toppled backwards and lay still.

Keill stepped past the crumpled forms of the two club-wielders and took hold of the collar of Crask's coverall, effortlessly jerking the bulky form to a sitting position.

'I want what information you have,' he said quietly, 'and I want it now.'

'You bust m' arm!' Crask groaned, almost sobbing.

Keill tightened his grip, twisting so the collar bit into the thick neck. 'Your neck will break as easily.'

'Don't – wait!' Crask shouted, half-choking. 'I'll tell y'!'

'Go on.' The steely grip eased a fraction.

'Don't really know much,' Crask mumbled.

Keill's other hand came round, palm under Crask's heavy jaw, bending the neck back. 'After all this, you had better know something,' he said grimly.

'Wait! All right!' Again the grip eased, and Crask, gasping, began to spill out words. 'Just bar-talk, see? Weeks back. When everybody was talkin' about your planet, wonderin' how it happened, lots of rumours.'

'What kind of rumours?'

'Just space talk. You know. One figures a sun flare, another figures a collision with somethin' from space. Nobody knows. Then one fella, freighterman, he says he's seen some legionaries. Two, three of 'em. An' they're like you – lookin' for others.'

'What did this freighterman say about them?'

'Not much. He didn't talk to them. One of them was a real big son – dangerous lookin'. But this fella, the freighterman, he heard that these legionaries were aimin' to set up a base somewhere.'

Urgency made Keill's grip tighten again on the collar. 'Where?'

'Listen, go easy, will y'?' Crask pawed weakly at the fierce grip. 'Somewhere out near Saltrenius. That's all he said – truth. Don't know nothin' more.'

Without a word Keill flung the man aside and turned to move swiftly towards his ship. Despite his control, his pulse had quickened, his eyes were bright, tendrils of hope rose within him. He had heard tales of legionaries being seen, had followed them all down to their ultimate dead ends. But this was different. A fixed base, of course! It was the right thing to do – and then from it send out the word to be picked up by any other survivors from Moros, to gather them in.

Above him the blunt wedge-shape of his ship loomed. He sprang up the ramp and through the hatch of the airlock, sealing it behind him ready for space. Strapping himself into the padded slingseat, he swiftly activated the control panel, feeding details into his guidance computer. Around him the life-support system hummed sweetly into action, and in moments the ship rose howling into the night, on a towering pillar of almost invisible energy.

As he hurtled through the territorial space of Coranex, Keill brought himself under control, regaining his calm, his patience. His eyes and hands automatically monitored the precision of his departure orbit, while his mind just as automatically sorted through the details of the journey ahead. He knew his fuel core was getting near to needing replenishment, but it would probably last. His air renewal, food concentrates and the rest would also hold out. Thankfully, he would need no stopovers till he reached the planet Saltrenius.

Idly he wondered why the group of legionaries – two? three? – would choose such a place. A sparsely inhabited world, in a minor system, well off the major spaceways. What could it offer? And who, he wondered, was the big legionary whom Crask's freighterman had described as 'dangerous looking'?

But Keill had learned long before the futility of asking

questions that could not be answered. Answers would come when he reached Saltrenius.

He had reached deep space now, the planet he had just left receding into a small disc of brightness in the rear viewscreen. The other screens, forward and side, presented the familiar panorama – the unnumbered points of light that made up mankind's Inhabited Galaxy.

Keill's fingertips issued more instructions to his computer, which searched its prodigious memory for the position of the planet Saltrenius, found it, and set its course.

On the viewscreens the points of light shimmered, blurred. The computer was obediently taking the ship out of planetary drive and into 'Overlight' – in which a ship could cross the breadth of the galaxy in only days.

The viewscreens went blank. A formless void gathered round Keill and his ship. In Overlight, he no longer existed in the normal universe. Moving unfathomable times faster than the speed of light, the ship had entered a *non-place*, leaving space and time behind it. Only Keill's inner time sense remained, to note the computer's estimate of arrival at Saltrenius in about ten hours.

He settled back against the slingseat, letting his eyes close wearily. It had been a long and active night – and somewhere, behind his rigid control, the pain still flamed and seared throughout his body.

Yet he felt a fierce gladness as sleep began to close round him. At least there was a chance now that he would find others of his kind, before he died. And perhaps then he would also find answers to *all* his questions. Even, if fortune willed it, a chance to wreak the bitter, hate-filled vengeance that blazed within him more fiercely than any physical pain.

But that thought, all thought, faded as he drifted into sleep. And with sleep, as if from the grey emptiness that surrounded his speeding ship, came the dreams.

chapter two

The dreams were fragmentary at first, as they always were. Broken, fleeting visions of a landscape – of a bleak and inhospitable world, dominated by chill expanses of desert, by towering ranges of rock-fanged mountains.

It was Keill Randor's world – the planet Moros, in the system of a white star on the outer reaches of the Inhabited Galaxy. A harsh world it was, a harsh life it gave to the space colonists who had made it their home so long ago, during the centuries of the Scattering – the time when the human race had spread itself out through the many millions of planets in the galaxy, to seek those thousands that could support human life.

Moros was one of them, for at least it had breathable air, with water and thin vegetation grudgingly available in its central regions. It also had a variety of its own life forms – the venomous reptiles of many weird shapes, the deadly sand cats, the huge, horned mammoths of the mountains, the tangled vine growths that fed on flesh – all as dangerous and threatening as the desert itself.

Yet they had survived, those early spacefarers – survived and adapted to their new home. And its rigours made them and their offspring tough, resourceful, self-reliant people, who even so had learned the need for order, stability and discipline in their lives. There was room for little else, from the beginning, if humans were to survive on Moros.

Yet the discipline was not *imposed*, from above. It was *accepted*, as a religion is accepted, by every human inhabitant of that world. It was taught to the children before they were weaned. It became a basic reality of life.

In the same way, as they learned to order and discipline

themselves, so the humans of Moros learned to fight to protect themselves. Fighting, against the alien beasts, the cruel environment, was also a reality of life, was essential for life itself. The people of Moros taught themselves and their children everything they needed to know for survival, in every kind of deadly circumstance. And that included a strict schooling in forms of self-defence and combat, unarmed or with a wide array of weaponry.

So the people lived, their numbers grew, even finding a share of contentment and satisfaction in the relentless hardships of their rugged, austere lives. But Moros was a poor planet, with little to offer the rest of the galaxy in trade. For centuries it remained mostly alone, unvisited. And all that time its people developed and refined their special way of life, becoming more fiercely independent, self-sufficient, at one with themselves. They also became a planetful of the most skilled, most effective fighting men and women in the galaxy.

Yet the people of Moros never lost that earliest sense of total commitment. In their world, *communality* ruled – cooperation, sharing, mutual aid and support. The people of Moros did not fight among themselves. All competition was relegated to an annual festival, the Martial Games. In their way of life, private greed, destructive ambition, selfish indifference to the needs of others – such anti-social, anti-survival ways were almost unknown.

Slowly, other human-inhabited planets in that region of the galaxy became aware of the uniqueness of Moros. And others saw what the people of Moros had not realized – that theirs was not truly a poor planet, for it had a special and valuable natural resource.

It had the martial skills of its population.

Gradually, the people of Moros were invited to use that resource, to trade with it as if it were minerals or food products. They took their skills out into the galaxy, small groups of fighting men and women, hired – at substantial sums – to fight in small wars on this planet or that. They became what,

20

in an ancient human language, had once been called *mercenaries*. But they felt no shame in doing so, nor was any put upon them.

They learned just how supremely skilled they were, compared to other soldiers in the Inhabited Worlds. And the rest of the galaxy learned as well. Soon more offers were coming in then could be accepted, and Moros began to know a measure of wealth.

With that income – held in common, like most property on the planet – the people of Moros acquired new, up-to-date equipment and weapons. They bought spaceships, from one-man fighters to vast battle cruisers, and created a formidable fleet. They visited other worlds, studied other advanced combat techniques and took them home for their people to master them. So they organized themselves into an armed force that could, if needed, include every adult on the planet. It was a force that became legendary throughout the galaxy.

The Legions of Moros.

Even then, even though any army needs carefully drawn lines and levels of command, the communal spirit of Moros was not impaired. Nor was the order and discipline: discord, slacking, disobedience were unknown, and would have been shocking notions to any legionary. In battle, some led and others followed, but they did so in order that every section and unit would operate like a finely tuned machine.

Otherwise the legionaries shared their lives as equals – working together, going into combat together, celebrating victories together.

And, in the end, dying together.

(Keill Randor's dream shifted, as it always did, and the broken, fleeting images gathered, held steady. From the depths of his sleeping darkness Keill moaned, as the dream-memory rose, clear and terrible – of the words he had heard from his ship's communicator that day . . .)

He had been sent, with the other one-person ships of his Strike Group, on a simple reconnaissance mission. But it was more than halfway across the galaxy, and in one of the most densely populated sectors, where human worlds and their stars clustered like – as the Morosian saying had it – sand fleas at an oasis.

Keill and his Group had come out of Overlight and were moving on ordinary planetary drive towards their objective – a small planet where a local war looked like expanding into a major conflict, and where the Legions had been offered a huge sum to join in on one side.

The Strike Group's mission was simply to gather data, to study the planet from orbit, to assess the war potential, to monitor broadcasts and so on. This data would help the Central Command of the Legions to decide whether to take up the offer.

For the Legions, by then, could pick and choose among contracts. And their ethic, born of their history, would not allow them to take the side of aggressors, or fanatics, or would-be exploiters.

Often they had fought, for less payment, on the side of those defending themselves against just such enemies. Often, indeed, the mere presence of the Legions on the side of the defenders had prevented an aggressor from ever launching a full-scale attack.

As the planet grew larger in their viewscreens, Keill and his group were checking their inter-ship communications link, preparing to slide into an orbit suitable for scanning the surface of this world. They were not advertising their presence, and hoped to go unnoticed – so Keill was mildly annoyed when he spotted a handful of silvery, tubular shapes rising towards his group through clouds beneath them. A subdued ripple of voices on the communicator showed that the rest of the group had also seen the other ships.

'Maybe they're friendly, maybe not,' Keill said to his group. 'We'll ease away on a new course and be ready for evasive action.'

His fingers moved over the controls, programming in the

new course that his group would pick up and follow. He kept his eyes firmly on the approaching ships, waiting for some sign of their intention, some communication from them.

As he watched, twin points of light glimmered from the tapering noses of each of the oncoming ships. Keill clenched his teeth angrily. It was all the sign he needed: he knew an ion-energy beam-gun when he saw one.

'They're firing,' he snapped into his communicator. 'Amateurs – they're way out of range still. Begin new course for evasive action.'

'Do we return fire?' The voice from the communicator was that of young Oni Wolda, Keill's next-in-command and his closest friend in the Strike Group. Her voice was calm, but with a faint note of eagerness that made Keill smile.

'No,' he said quickly. 'We're not here to fight. Evasive action will take us far enough out for Overlight – that'll lose them. Then we'll report back.'

Again he made his course corrections on the control panel. Then he added, 'I'll drop back into rear position and find out who this gun-happy bunch belongs to.'

But before any of his group could acknowledge, his communicator hummed for an instant and then spoke, not in the voices of his friends but in the abrasive, metallic tone of a long-range communication.

URGENT MESSAGE FROM HOME PLANET – MESSAGE FROM HOME PLANET.

Keill sat up, startled. Messages seldom came from Moros to legionaries on a mission, unless the legionaries themselves first made contact, to report or to call for reinforcements in an emergency.

The communicator seemed to have plucked the word from his thoughts.

EMERGENCY MESSAGE ALL LEGIONARIES – EMERGENCY ALL LEGIONARIES

PLANET UNDER ATTACK BY UNKNOWN FORCES

ALL LEGIONARIES RETURN TO MOROS AT ONCE – REPEAT

Shock turned Keill's blood to ice. Moros under attack? It had never happened – not in all the centuries. Who would be foolhardy enough to attack the home world of the galaxy's most renowned fighting force?

But the words had been spoken, and had to be true.

'Emergency procedure!' he shouted. 'Prepare for Overlight at my signal!'

It was risky, entering Overlight that close to a planet's gravitational pull, but there was no choice. *At once*, the terrible order had said – and Keill had no intention of arriving too late, if only by seconds, to be of use.

His fingers flowed over the controls, making his ship ready for Overlight. His hand was hovering over the activator, his mouth beginning to form the order to his group, when his ship jerked and leaped beneath him like a startled animal.

Furious, he glanced at his rear viewscreen. He had nearly forgotten the other ships, in the shock of the message from Moros. And because he had dropped back into the rear position of his group, he had come within range of the others' beam-guns. One of them had got lucky: he had been hit.

It would take time before his computer could produce a damage report – but he could feel his ship slowing, juddering slightly. Behind him the attacking ships were closing the gap, still firing wildly.

All he could do was to take his group into safety – and hope desperately that it was not his Overlight drive that had been damaged.

'Ready to enter Overlight,' he snapped, '*now*!'

His hand punched the activator – and the formless void gathered him in.

Though in Overlight, a ship seemed to be at rest, motionless, while leaping across the unimaginable distances, there were many special stresses and pressures within the void. It was a place from which a damaged ship might very well never emerge.

So Keill sweated and waited for the computer's damage report. It came in seconds, but they seemed like hours.

Damage recorded from energy beam contact   Hull sector eight-A

Keill's heart sank. It was a forward sector of the ship's hull, holding some of the weaponry and much of the navigational equipment. The computer went on, confirming his fears:

Hull buckled but unbroken and holding   One forward beam-gun inoperable   Navigation system planetary drive inoperable

Keill reached for the computer keys. *Report status of Overlight drive*, he ordered, *and other systems*.

The obedient computer replied at once. *Overlight drive undamaged   Other weapons systems undamaged   Life support systems undamaged   Communications system undamaged*

Relief left Keill sagging back into his slingseat. The Overlight was intact. The emptiness beyond space would not claim him.

He touched the keys again. *Estimate repair time for planetary drive and damaged weapons*, he ordered.

E R T for damaged beam-gun nil   Weapon not repairable   Full replacement required   E R T for navigation system six hours

He cursed softly. Six hours! He begrudged every moment that he was in Overlight – yet now he would need to work for six hours before his planetary drive could take him to his planet's aid. And even then he would arrive with part of his armament out of action.

But there was nothing he could do. No one went outside a ship in Overlight. No repairs could be begun until he emerged into normal space, many hours from then.

Gritting his teeth, he fingered the keys again. At least he could occupy himself usefully during the agonising wait – as legionaries were trained to do. *Begin full check of all equipment and systems*, he ordered, *other than damaged sector*.

And he turned his full, disciplined concentration on to the laborious routine check, while his crippled ship plunged ahead through an emptiness as unknowable as the future.

chapter three

(The dream-memories were gathering pace now, and Keill writhed in his sleep, powerless to stop his unconscious mind from forming the images that he had re-lived so often before, in horror and despair . . .)

The time of waiting had ground finally to its end, and the ships of Keill's Strike Group came out of Overlight. They had re-entered normal space at a maximal orbital distance: legionaries did not plunge blindly into confrontations without knowing what they were confronting.

But, as Keill studied the face of the planet Moros looming and filling his viewscreen, all seemed puzzlingly calm and normal. There was a faint, hazy aura round the image of the planet, but Keill discounted that as a possible minor malfunction of the screen, to do with the damage his ship had suffered. Certainly his ship sensors reported no other ships of any sort within the planet's range, and no form of attack going on.

At least, then, his Group seemed to be in no visible danger. So he sent the other ships curving away in their approach path to the planet's surface. And he dragged on a spacesuit, trudged out on to the ship's exterior, and began with desperate speed to work on his damaged navigation system.

The computer's estimate was accurate: more than two hours later, the work was only half done. Keill sweated and fumed as he laboured – yet his hands remained deft, controlled, and his concentration remained complete.

Until it was broken by the warning, from the computer in his helmet communicator, that the sensors had picked up a lone ship, approaching fast from the planet's surface.

Keill was back at his controls in seconds, readying his undamaged weapons, examining in his screen the glinting speck of metal that was sweeping towards him.

Then it was close enough for him to recognize the blue circlet embossed on its side, and his battle-readiness relaxed. It was one of the ships from his own Strike Group – the ship of Oni Wolda.

Keill waited tensely while the other ship slid into parallel orbit. Then, as he expected, the communicator came to life. It did so with a cracking buzz that indicated strong interference – which might have puzzled Keill, had not the words themselves driven all other thoughts from his mind.

'Oni Wolda to Keill Randor   Oni to Keill   The planet is dead   The whole planet   Every person   Every living thing   Nothing left alive on the surface'

The horror took hold of Keill, stopping his breathing, seeming to squeeze his heart in its icy grip. Even the communicator paused, as if Oni herself could not find words to follow the enormity of that statement.

'Attack came with no warning   Unknown radiation released over entire planet   Central Command set up a beacon, before they died, to warn groups like ours   But too much interference   Too weak   We did not pick up the warning till too late'

Too late? The words echoed in Keill's shocked mind as Oni went on.

'Keill   Pain began in us almost at once   Knew what it meant Nothing to be done   Rest of Group went on to land   To die on Moros with the others   I came to stop you   Don't know if you're safe even this far out'

Keill's face twisted, his body hunched, aching, torn with a grief that was inconsolable, a fury that was beyond bearing. Oni's voice went on, though Keill had already anticipated the rest of the terrible message.

'This is a recording   Keill I am dying too   Will be dead when you hear this   Go Overlight and get away   Do not approach planet Nothing to be seen or done   Save yourself if you still can   Warn other legionaries if there are any alive

*'And if you live try to find who did this evil   Avenge us Keill
Avenge the murder of Moros'*

For a long time – too long – Keill sat motionless, while grief
and horror and savage rage tore at his sanity. But in the end
some of the strength of his mind and will returned. He forced
his numb fingers to the controls, and sent his ship into Overlight.

Only moments later he re-emerged into normal space, far
beyond the outer reaches of the solar system that contained his
now dead and deadly world. There he set up a beacon of his
own, instructing his computer to broadcast a message on a
wide and regular sweep, which would be picked up by any
other late-coming legionaries and save them from the death-
trap that awaited them on Moros.

Then he went doggedly, automatically, back to the labour of
finishing the repairs to his planetary drive.

The work was completed quickly. But even then Keill did
not move away. Blank and unmoving, he sat and stared out at
space, unaware of the passage of time, trying to come to terms
with the monstrous reality that had so nearly unhinged his
mind. Several times he toyed with the thought that Oni
might have been wrong – or that it had not been Oni at all,
but some enemy's trick – and that he should after all return
and descend to Moros to see for himself.

But he always managed to resist the impulse. It had been
Oni's ship, and there had been no time for an enemy to use it
for an elaborate deception. And he knew by instinct somehow
that her dying message had been real, and true.

Meanwhile his communicator tirelessly broadcast his warning – but received no reply. And a fearful thought began to
grow in him – that there might never be a reply.

What if his Strike Group had been the farthest from home of
any unit of the Legions? What if they had been the very last to
arrive, and last to descend into the fatal aura of the radiation?
That would make him . . .

The last legionary.

But as the hours passed, something else – not intuition but physical sensation, from within his body – told him that, even if it were true, that he was the only one left, it was not likely to matter to him for very long.

It seemed to emanate from his very bones – faint, but tangible and definite.

A deep-lying sensation of burning pain.

Oni's gallant attempt to save him had not worked. Even as far from the planet as he had been, some radiation must have reached him. A weaker dose, though, which would let him live a while yet.

How long he would have was not the most important question in his mind. Far more urgent were the questions that bore with them the full power of his sorrow and his rage: *who* and *why*?

But the fact that he would have only a limited time to seek the answers restored him to himself, a legionary again, and galvanized him into action.

He turned his ship away from the solar system of Moros, and began the slow, frustrating process of his search.

From world to world he moved, watching, listening, asking his careful questions. Whenever he was in space, his communicator kept up its patient broadcast. And the weeks, the months, passed uselessly.

Whoever had attacked Moros had covered their tracks well. The news of the planet's destruction spread round the Inhabited Worlds quickly, as such news always did – but Keill could find not one grain of fact or hope within the quantities of speculation and rumour. So he had come to Coranex, just one more stop in his random, desperate planet-hopping – knowing with bitter rage how rapidly his time was running out.

The pain within him had grown steadily more fierce, though

in the legionary's way he had kept it firmly under control, so that no one would have guessed that he was not in perfect health. But at last, on one of his earlier planetary stops, he had spent a few galacs to consult a space medic.

The medic made exhaustive tests. And the gloom that settled on his brow was enough to tell Keill the results.

The radiation – from some altered isotope unrecognized by either Keill or the medic – had settled in Keill's bones. There it was creating cellular changes and breakdowns that were surely, inevitably, killing him.

A month more, the medic had said. Two at the most.

More than half of that month had passed by the time he made planetfall on Coranex. Keill had almost begun looking forward to the end – not only as a release from the pain. It would also release him from the dreams that came to torment his nights, in which he re-lived the terrible day when he thought he was rushing to his planet's aid and found he had come to join it only in death.

And it would release him from the despair which came with the growing realization that his search for other legionary survivors seemed more and more hopeless.

But now . . . hope had revived. If the man called Crask had been speaking the truth, he was only hours from a meeting with other survivors, and perhaps some answers to the questions that plagued him as fiercely as the pain.

(The flavour of that anticipation reached into the dream, filled it, changed its nature. The tense movements of his closed eyes dwindled as the dream images fragmented again and scattered. For the first time in weeks, Keill sank deeper into a peaceful, undisturbed sleep. And his ship plunged on through nothingness, towards a planet called Saltrenius.)

The spaceport at Saltrenius might have been the port at Coranex – the same plasticrete surface, scarred and crumbled here and there from shoddy maintenance and the batterings of a thousand ships – the same low, shabby buildings where bored officials scanned identification, took details, yawningly accepted landing fees.

Even the town clustered near the port might have been transplanted from Coranex and all the other small, unimportant worlds like it. Of course there were differences: the shape of the buildings, the appearance and dress of the people. Saltrenius was grimier than most worlds, for much of the planet was devoted to gathering and processing a dusty residue from the bark of a native plant, used on many worlds in medical compounds. The dust, Keill found, was everywhere – especially, it seemed, on the usual assortment of dingy buildings devoted to the less choosy pleasure-seekers among space travellers.

This time, though, Keill avoided those streets. He was looking for a different source of information – local facts, this time, rather than space talk. Every world naturally had its own forms of communications media – holo-screen or the more out-dated ultravid. The media people were the ones most likely to know what he needed to know.

A few questions, and he located the building he wanted, which housed the local office of the communications network. Squat, grey and dull the building was, and Keill spared it hardly a glance. A few more questions, a few galacs changing hands, and a secretary was going in search of a network newsman. 'Just the man you want,' Keill had been told. 'Knows everything going on in Saltrenius.'

Only minutes later Keill was sitting in a noisy, crowded reception area, with a beaker of some unidentifiable fluid before him, while across the table a grey old man who said his name was Xann Exur was gulping a similar beakerful with every sign of deep enjoyment.

At last the beaker was set down, empty. Keill, his own still untasted, signalled a bartender for another, then looked hopefully at the old man.

Exur wiped his lips, loose grey flesh wobbling at jowl and

throat. 'Sure I can help you, boy. Glad to. Always thought well of the Legions – terrible thing that happened.'

Keill nodded, waiting.

The old man leaned forward. In his eyes shone the eternal hope of a professional newsman scenting a story. 'Any ideas yourself how it happened?'

Keill shook his head. 'If you can tell me what I want to know, I might be on the way to some ideas. But I haven't much time.'

Exur looked disappointed. 'Ah well, imagine it'll all come out someday.' His second drink came, and he was about to gulp it in the wake of the first when Keill leaned forward and took hold of the skinny wrist. The grip was light, but the old man did not fail to sense the steely strength within those fingers.

'I said I haven't much time,' Keill said quietly.

'Oh, right, sure,' Exur said rapidly. 'Like I said, glad to help. What's happened is this . . .'

Keill released his grip and listened patiently as the old man told his rambling tale. Three men in legionary uniform had come to Saltrenius, a month or so earlier. They had picked up supplies, and had spent some time in the town, where Exur had heard of their presence and had spoken to them.

The three had confirmed that Moros was destroyed, and that they might be the last living members of the Legions. But in case they weren't, they had been spreading the word round the spaceways. They were planning to set up a base, so that if there were other survivors they too could make their way to Saltrenius and join their fellows.

'Did they say why they had chosen this place?' Keill asked.

'Nope. And I didn't press them. They didn't mind talking to me, telling me their story, but they didn't like too many questions. Especially the big fella.'

'But did you find out where this base is?'

'Sure.' The old man grinned, pleased with himself. 'On Creffa.'

'Creffa?'

Exur waved a skinny hand in the air. 'One of our moons. Saltrenius's got two.'

Keill looked baffled. Why a moon? Why Saltrenius at all? And the old man read his expression correctly.

'Yep, I wondered why Creffa too. Didn't like to ask, by then, but they told me. There's an old space-dome out there, built when we were exploring the moons, years back. They're fixing it up to be their base. Guess they like to keep themselves to themselves.'

Keill was still slightly puzzled, but at least that part made sense. Moros had, after all, been *attacked*. The attacker, whoever it might be, was still around somewhere. A handful of legionaries would think first of setting up a base that was at once remote and defensible. A dome on an airless moon might do very well.

'Then they're still there?' he asked.

'Sure,' Exur said. 'Been seen just recently, down here. They come down now and then to pick up stuff they need.'

'And there's no doubt in your mind that they're legionaries?'

'Well, they said they were, that's all I can say. And they were wearing uniforms like yours, with that blue circle thing.' The old man paused. 'All except that big fella . . .'

'What about him?'

Exur chortled. 'He didn't seem to like clothes too much. Oh, he had on the pants and boots like yours – but he always went round stripped to the waist. Still, reckon if I had muscles like him I'd show 'em off too.'

Keill frowned, then reached up to undo the top fasteners of his tunic. From round his neck he drew a light metal chain, from which dangled a disc of hard plastic. He held out the disc in the palm of his hand.

'Was the big man wearing one of these?' he asked.

Exur studied the disc with interest. Around its edge was the brilliant blue circlet that was the Legion insignia. Within it, embedded deep in the plastic, were coded shapes – which, to other legionraies, would reveal Keill's place of origin on Moros and his rank in the Legions. There was also a tiny but perfectly clear three-dimensional colour image of Keill's face.

'Now I never saw one of those before,' Exur said. 'Identification, is it?'

Keill nodded. 'Every legionary has one. And each disc is chemically tuned to the physical make-up of its owner. No one can wear anyone else's, and they're hard to forge. Here.'

He placed the disc in the old man's hand. At once the sky-blue circlet began to alter – darkening, shifting, until in seconds it glowed a deep, almost angry red.

Exur stared, fascinated. 'Nice bit of work, that. Interesting.' He handed back the disc – which returned to its normal blue as Keill took it and slipped the chain round his neck again. 'Anyway,' the old man went on, 'the big fella definitely didn't have one of them.'

'Are you sure?'

'Course. Man's got a chest like a wall. Didn't have any decorations on it.' Again a pause. 'Except for the markings.'

'Markings?'

'Yep – like tattoos, maybe, or like scars, except they were too neat and even. Raised ridges of skin, like – one round his neck, one round his belly.' A skinny finger demonstrated. 'Legionaries have them, too?'

'No,' Keill said thoughtfully. 'Nothing like that.'

The old man's eyes sparkled with curiosity. 'Are you thinking that these fellas aren't real legionaries?'

'I don't know what I'm thinking. But this big man *did* say he was ... ?'

'Yep. He did most of the talking. Lot of laughing, too. Not very pleasant. Made me downright nervous – I was glad to get away, I can tell you.'

Keill nodded, and stood up. 'I'm grateful for your help, Xann Exur – more than I can say. I wish I'd met you sooner.

I'm deeply in your debt, and I doubt if I'll be able to repay it.' As if to echo his words, the pain stabbed through him more savagely than ever.

But the old man noticed nothing. 'My pleasure, son, and my job. I'm a newsman, and you could be news. If you find out those fellas are fakes, let me know, will you?'

Keill smiled grimly. 'If they really *are* legionaries, I'll let you know. If they're not – then I'll probably be too busy, for a while.'

chapter four

Keill went back to the spaceport as rapidly as he could, fighting
to keep his inner calm and control despite the puzzlement and
urgency that chafed at him. Questions upon questions, mysteries upon mysteries heaped themselves up in his mind, with
one especially looming largest and most disturbing.

Were the three men legionaries?

If they were, a huge range of possibilities – and other questions – would open up, mainly to do with the murder of Moros
and the unknown destroyer.

But if they were *not* . . . then what were they up to?

And what could he do about it?

He knew it would be a journey of less than an hour from
lift-off to landing on the moon Creffa, where some at least of
these questions would be answered. But he knew also that he
would resent the passage of each one of those minutes.

Time was now his most precious possession. Every minute
gone was another step towards the day – soon now, as the
medic had said – when the pain would grow strong enough to
batter down his iron control, when the radiation within him
would overwhelm and quench his life.

Every delay, however brief, was a robbery – making it even
less likely that he would find the answers he needed before
that final moment came.

So another man – a man without the inner discipline of a
legionary – might have gone wholly berserk with fury and
frustration if he had found what Keill found at the spaceport.

He could not enter his ship.

Someone had fixed an electromolecular seal across the hatch

of the airlock – a plain metal band, but as secure and unopenable a fastening as could be found in the galaxy.

Someone did not want Keill Randor to leave.

The senior security officer of the spaceport was not inclined to be helpful.

'Can't tell you any more.' The official was a grey-faced Saltrenian with a permanently sour expression, made sourer by the visible anger behind Keill's questions. 'Like I said, official orders came – for me to seal your ship and give you that.'

He pointed to the paper Keill held. What it contained had only served to deepen the mystery. The paper had announced, unnecessarily, the official sealing of his ship. And it had 're-quested' Keill to take a room at a spacer hostel near the port, and wait there to be contacted on 'a matter of some urgency'.

The paper did not say who would make the contact. But it was signed by the Deputy Co-ordinator of the Saltrenian Civil Control.

'I've broken no laws on this planet,' Keill said fiercely. 'I've been here barely a day – now I simply want to leave. Peacefully. Your people have no right to stop me.'

'I've got my orders,' said the officer, 'and that's all there is.' He let one hand stray meaningfully near the weapon at his side – another needle-gun, Keill had seen. 'If you want to argue, and talk about rights, take it up with the CC. Your ship stays sealed till they say otherwise.'

'I will.' Keill turned away, then looked back and said almost casually, 'But you have the key here?'

'No concern of yours where it is,' the official growled. 'Not till the CC says otherwise.'

Keill nodded and left the room, hiding his grim satisfaction. Before the officer had replied, his eyes had briefly flicked sideways, towards a locked metal cabinet against one wall. The man had probably not even realized that he had made the movement. But it was all Keill needed.

Leaving the spaceport building, he glanced for a moment across the empty plasticrete towards where his ship stood. The distance was considerable, for the main pads were well away from the buildings. But Keill's eyes could make out enough details – and what he saw made him stop abruptly and stare.

Four men had gathered around his ship. One of the men was a uniformed spaceport security guard. Two of the others wore different uniforms, which Keill recognized at once despite their abundant covering of Saltrenian dust. Legion uniforms.

And the fourth man . . .

At least a head taller than the others, massively built. And naked to the waist.

The three men seemed to be examining Keill's ship, while chatting with the security guard. And the big man was laughing.

Keill had taken three running strides across the plasticrete before a sharp voice behind him brought him up short.

'Randor!'

He turned and saw the senior security officer in the doorway.

'My orders say you're to be kept away from that ship,' he growled. 'I've put a man on it. Don't get any ideas.'

Anger swelled within Keill, but his voice was cool. 'There are some men out there,' he said, pointing, 'who I must talk to.'

The officer narrowed his eyes and peered.

'Do you know them?' Keill asked quickly.

'Yes – think so.' The officer nodded. 'Those're the legionaries who've set up on Creffa.' He looked down at Keill, some of the sourness leaving his eyes. 'Guess I can understand you wanting to see them. Go on, then – just stay away from the ship.'

Keill whirled and ran. But in that moment – whether by some instinct or accident – the half-naked giant in the distance turned, and caught sight of the figure sprinting towards them.

Immediately the huge man spoke to his companions – who turned, looked, and began to walk away. They did not seem to hurry, but they did not stroll. And it was only a short distance to the bulky cylinder of the space cruiser that stood waiting on the next pad.

Despite his desperate speed, Keill had covered only half the distance when the three men vanished through the airlock of their ship. But not before the big man had paused for one more look back at Keill.

Keill was able to see him more closely then. He could see the vast muscles swelling beneath bronze skin. And, faintly, the peculiar markings that the newsman had mentioned – the narrow, raised bands encircling the thick throat, the ridged belly.

He could also see the mockery behind the big man's laughter.

Then the hatch closed, and Keill was left to watch helplessly as, in seconds, the cruiser lifted away.

He might have screamed with rage and desperation. He might have rushed to his own ship to tear with crazed hopelessness at the unbreakable seal.

Instead, he turned on his heel and walked calmly away to find the offices of the Civil Control.

The afternoon was beginning to wane by the time he had found his way. And there, too, he met frustration. The uniformed Civil Control officer in the front office was less sour than the man at the spaceport, but no more helpful. He knew nothing about the seal on Keill's ship, or the reasons for it. The Deputy Co-ordinator was not available. No one else would be able to tell Keill anything.

'Why don't you just do what the letter says?' the officer suggested. 'Go to the hostel and wait. The Deputy will be along. It's all you can do.'

Again the helplessness swept over Keill. Again deep anger

throbbed within him. Again he was icily impassive as he turned and left the offices.

Through the gathering dusk he located the spacer hostel that the official letter had named, and took a room – indifferent to its drab, functional, none-too-clean interior. And there he waited.

It was all he could do.

He was standing at the open window of his second-floor room, ignoring the dust-laden breeze, staring out at the two moons that had risen into the night sky of Saltrenius, when the knock came. He flung open the door before the startled man who had knocked had even begun to lower his hand.

The Deputy Co-ordinator was a civil servant through and through. His name was Shenn, and he was small, grey as any Saltrenian, precise in movements and speech. Less small and less neat were the two large uniformed men behind him, with the metallic 'CC' gleaming on cap and collar. But the Deputy left them outside, at the door, and even managed a precise little smile as he greeted Keill.

The smile faded somewhat when Keill told him, in terms all the more unnerving for the frozen, knife-edged tone of voice, what he thought of his situation, the CC, and Saltrenius in general.

'I fear I can explain very little to you,' Shenn said at last. 'Orders came to me that you were not to leave the planet.'

'Orders from whom?' Keill demanded.

'Higher authority. In the government.'

'And why,' Keill wanted to know, 'should your government want to keep me here against my will?'

'It seems that they received a request.' Shenn quickly lifted a small hand before Keill could interrupt. 'I do not know its origin – it is not for me to know. But someone of, apparently, great importance, off-world, is sending a message to Saltrenius for you. On a matter of grave urgency. We were requested to ensure that you remained, till this message arrives.'

'Nothing more?'

'Nothing.'

'No idea what this mysterious message is about, or who sent it?'

'None.'

'Then,' Keill said, 'you are wasting my time.'

He took hold of the Deputy before the little man could even draw breath to shout. One hand over the mouth to silence him, one hand clamped on his neck, thumb pressing the carotid artery that feeds blood to the brain. In seconds Deputy Shenn crumpled into unconsciousness, with not a sound to alert the waiting guards outside.

Keill dumped the man on the bed, knowing that he would awaken, unharmed, almost as quickly as he had collapsed. But for a second he paused, curiosity tugging at him. He wanted very much to know what lay behind the sealing of his ship, and who was the mystery person with so much influence, who was sending an unknown message. Yet he wanted even more to get off-planet, to find the three men who said they were legionaries.

The lack of time demanded that a choice must be made. And Keill's choice was obvious.

Perhaps he would try, afterwards, to contact Saltrenius and learn more about this mystery. If there was time. If he was still alive to contact anyone.

Meanwhile . . .

He eased himself out of the window, and glanced down. A gloomy passageway ran behind the hostel, filled with stenches and shadows. He moved out on to the sill – then halted.

An odd sound above him, like a rustle of cloth.

He glanced up quickly. Nothing but the blank edge of the roof, the night sky above it.

A legionary's training covers a great many physical skills, including knowing how to fall – even two storeys. He took the impact with legs well bent – rolled, and bounced to his feet again, casually rubbing one slightly bruised hip. Then he slid into a shadow, and was gone.

*

Spaceport security guards on minor planets do not have a difficult job. The owners of spaceships pay a small fee for the use of the port – a larger fee if passengers or freight handling are involved. But shipowners are responsible for protecting their own ships, usually managed with little more than some advanced technology in the locking mechanisms on both entrances and control panels. Few spaceships were stolen, in Keill's day: they were too easy to trace, to difficult to re-sell. Saltrenius had not had a spaceship theft in living memory.

So the guard on the perimeter of the central port buildings might have been forgiven for being half asleep, lulled by the unbroken silence and darkness around him. He might not even have felt the blow that deepened his doze into unconsciousness.

Keill lowered the guard's body to the ground, listening carefully to the man's breathing. He had struck with precision at the base of the skull, using only the tips of stiffened fingers, for he was not there to kill. Even so, some people have thinner skulls than others – and he was glad to hear the guard begin softly snoring.

He slipped the guard's pistol from its holster – a needle-gun, as he had hoped – and snapped it open, sniffing at the points of the tiny projectiles within it. Also as he had hoped, the guards used anaesthetic in their needlers. They, too, were not there to kill.

Like a shadow himself he moved through shadow towards his goal – the office of the senior security man, he with the sour expression. A dimly lit window drew him. Peering carefully in, he saw one guard, seated at the central desk with his back to the door, chewing at a handful of some nameless Saltrenian confection.

Keill ghosted to the door, opened it without a sound. Even the needle-gun seemed to whisper as he fired it. The guard, mouth still full, sagged forward onto the desk.

The metal cabinet – at which the senior officer had taken his giveaway look – was securely shut, with some form of electronic combination lock. The cabinet was sheet metal, a sturdy alloy. Keill stepped a pace away, took a deep breath, another.

Then he leaped, and drove a booted foot at full stretch into the centre of the cabinet door.

The blow had every gram of his weight perfectly poised and delivered behind it. It also had all the pent-up frustration, anger, desperation and urgency that had accompanied Keill throughout the whole of his day on Saltrenius.

The metal cabinet boomed hollowly. And the door seemed to fold inwards, as if it had developed new hinges down its centre.

Keill stood silent for a moment, listening. But the sound, loud enough in the enclosed room, would not have carried far outside. And more than one guard must have been feeling sleepy that night. No voices were raised, no footsteps began, no alarm sounded.

He turned back to the cabinet. On one side of the door, the electronic lock had held. On the other side, the door had been completely ripped off its hinges. In a moment Keill had pulled aside the crumpled metal and was rummaging through the shelves. In another moment a thin strip of light metal lay in his hand.

The key to the seal that held his ship prisoner.

Then he was outside again, circling, more silent than the dust that swirled softly in the air. He approached his ship from the rear, rounded it cautiously. The lone guard was at least wakeful, but when he saw Keill he could not decide for an instant whether to shout or to reach for his pistol. Keill shot him before he could make up his mind.

While he was dragging the unconscious man to safety, well away from the energy blast of his lift-off, Keill heard a sound, on the threshold of audibility. Like the sound he had heard at the hostel – a soft rustle, as if of cloth. He spun round, pistol ready – but saw nothing, except his waiting ship and swirls of soft dust. Carefully, warily, he circled his ship. Nothing. The plasticrete was bare, deserted, as far as he could see in the darkness.

Quickly he returned to the seal, slipping in the key, catching the band of heavy metal as it fell away, opening the airlock hatch, moving swiftly in . . .

The sound again. Behind him. Not a rustle this time – more like a cloth flapping in the wind.

He was quick enough to turn, quick enough to glimpse the shape that hovered outside – like a wide sheet, like a sail, blackly silhouetted against the star-filled sky.

Then the needle bit into his neck, and it seemed that all the shadows in the world rose to engulf him in darkness.

part two
The hidden asteroid

chapter five

He opened his eyes slowly, his mind sluggish, resisting wake-fulness. The messages from his senses were coming to him slowly, as if from a great distance, with difficulty.

The first message they sent was frightening. He was totally immobilized. He could not move a single muscle in his body except those around his eyes and mouth.

The second message was reassuring. He still had feeling in his body – he was not paralysed. Instead, something was con-straining him, something that clung to every centimetre of his skin except his face, preventing even the smallest movement.

The third message was unbelievable. Though he could not move, though his mind was far from clear, though he felt an immense weariness throughout his entire being, so that even moistening his lips with his tongue was an effort – despite all this, he felt wonderful.

The pain had gone.

The lancing fire that had seared every cell in the depths of his body, through every waking minute of the months past . . . Gone.

Unless, of course, he was dreaming again. Or perhaps delirious, in the final stages of the death that the pain had been a prelude to.

He rolled his eyes, up, down, sideways, to the limits of his peripheral vision. He saw the plain walls and ceiling of an un-remarkable room, with cheerful diffuse lighting. He noted that he was not lying flat on his back but propped up, half-reclin-ing, on some padded surface contoured to fit his body per-fectly.

He saw all that, but it was overridden by the shock of having seen himself.

He was entirely covered by a garment that clung like a second skin, which was certainly what held him immobile. It was silvery, shiny, and apparently without a seam. From many points on the garment – and so, presumably, from Keill's body, though he felt no discomfort – sprouted a huge array of tubes and wires, like the tendrils of some wild alien growth. The tubes and wires led on each side to a variety of complicated machinery, none of which seemed familiar to Keill in any way.

It was no dream, he decided. And it was an odd, unlikely scene for a delirium to shape. But then – *what was it*?

At that moment a voice spoke in the room. A firm male voice, with a note of friendliness, even kindliness, that seemed to come from everywhere.

'Are you awake, Keill Randor?'

Keill struggled in his throat to find his voice, found only a whisper. 'Who are you?'

The voice did not return at once. When it did, it seemed slightly muffled, as if the speaker had turned aside, addressing someone other than Keill.

'Amazing powers of recuperation . . . He shouldn't have wakened for days yet.'

'Days?' Keill whispered.

The voice replied at full volume again, but with an extra firmness. 'It is too soon, Keill Randor, for you to ask questions or receive answers. You will sleep again now, and we will speak later when you are entirely restored.'

Keill fought his voice into a desperate croak. 'Who are you? What are you? *What are you doing to me*?'

There was a pause. 'Very well, I see that those questions deserve some answer.' The voice grew even kindlier. 'My name is Talis, though that will mean little to you. I am a man, much as yourself, if a good deal older.' A chuckle. 'And what we are doing, Keill Randor, is saving your life.'

Keill wanted to cry out, wanted to scream questions, but his mind was a darkening jumble, unable to focus on words or their meanings, and he knew that one of the tubes in his eerie garment had slid a drug into his veins. He struggled with numbing lips, with the spreading blankness in his mind, and mumbled the only question he could manage.

'*Why*?'

He was not sure he had heard the answer, as he drifted into sleep. But it had sounded like—

'Because you are needed.'

He opened his eyes slowly, as before. But sensation flooded in upon him. His mind was not dulled this time, but alert, functioning, with a strange extra feeling of being marvellously refreshed.

And there was still no pain.

Yet his body was behaving in a disturbing way. He still could not move his head or limbs, still felt himself gripped and held in the half-lifted position – but every muscle was quivering, uncontrollably.

He glanced round, and down at himself, the memory of his previous awakening complete. He was no longer wearing the silvery garment. Instead, a light covering had been drawn over him, up to his neck. Beneath it, he knew he was naked. And he was still lying on the same padded bed, deeply contoured to fit the shape of his body exactly.

It was the contours of the bed that gripped him, and that were trembling – vibrating over the whole surface of his body. Relaxing with relief, he saw that it was an advanced form of massage unit, designed to maintain muscle tone and circulation in an immobilized patient.

He remembered the mysterious voice that had spoken to him. It had made clear that he would sleep for days. So he must have lain on that bed for a long time in the restrictions of the strange garment. The massage unit would have kept his muscles from weakening and deteriorating too much.

How weak he might be remained to be seen. It was not the

most important of the questions that clamoured in his mind. But it was probably the only one that he could answer for himself.

He inhaled deeply, aware that his body was relaxed, but testing the relaxation, letting it spread through every muscle, out of the centre of his being. Then he concentrated on his right arm, gathering his energies, focusing them, channelling them to that arm, building the power within it to a higher and higher peak . . .

Then, with a fierce exhalation, he released that power.

His arm ripped free of the constriction.

It was a small triumph, but an important first step – to regaining control over his own person, to putting an end to his time of lying trapped like a swaddled baby, while unknown people and strange machines did whatever they wished with him.

Yet he found that he was bathed in sweat after the exertion, and his free arm was oddly heavy. He let it fall on the outside of the covering, reaching again for the inner relaxation, knowing that he would need to rest awhile before trying to summon the power to free his other arm.

At that point a human figure appeared – materialized, from empty air – before him.

And the voice that Keill had heard before spoke again, still from no specific point within the room.

'Quite astonishing,' it said. 'You should not be at all strong enough, yet, to break free of the unit.'

Keill said nothing. Around him the massage unit's vibrations dwindled and stopped, and its grip on his body eased. It became merely a comfortably contoured bed, and Keill could move again. He began making small, minimal movements, stretching and twisting, testing the state of his body, while warily studying the figure that had appeared so suddenly.

An unadorned robe covered all of the figure's body, and extended into a heavy cowl, or hood, that was pulled forward so that the face was obscured in shadow. But from the posture of the figure, which was seated on a tall, plain chair, and the size and shape of the hands, Keill could see that he was in the presence of someone thin, elderly and probably male.

But then he saw that he was not actually in the *presence* of the figure. The angles of the shadowings and the faint haziness of outline told him that he was looking at a holo-image. Which explained the sudden materialization, and the apparently dis-embodied voice.

'Do not be alarmed, Keill Randor. You are not among enemies.'

'Who are you?' Keil said sharply, glad to find that his voice was working normally. 'What am I doing here?'

'You asked those questions before – do you remember?' said the voice. 'I am Talis, who spoke to you when you awoke prematurely ...'

'I remember,' Keill replied. 'But you told me little, and ex-plained nothing. Now I want explanations.'

'That is why I am here,' said the kindly voice. 'But tell me first how you feel.'

'I feel weak, as you must surely know,' Keill said brusquely. 'But everything seems to be functional. And the pain is gone.'

'Yes – we have removed the radiation from your body. Soon you will be fully restored to your normal state of health – which, it seems, is quite remarkable.'

'If that is so,' Keill said slowly, 'then I will owe you a debt that I can never repay. And I will want to know all the more who you are, and why this is happening.'

'Just so,' said the figure. 'There is much to tell you. There is much also that you cannot be told. But I will explain what I can.'

The figure settled back in its chair, folding its long hands, and continued.

'I am one of a group of people, mostly old dodderers like myself—' the warm voice chuckled as before—'who can im-modestly call themselves some of the leading intellects of the Inhabited Worlds. Most of us are scientists of one sort or another. You would doubtless recognize many of our names, if you were ever to know them.'

'You told me your name,' Keill interjected.

'Talis is the name I use now. It is not my true name – and that I cannot tell you.'

Keill shrugged and remained silent, while the image of the old man called Talis went on. He told Keill how most of the individuals in the group had known each other for a long time, had often worked together, conferring over problems of far-reaching importance round the galaxy. More and more they had been invited to work on specific problems by governments of different planets, here and there – because they were able to bring a vast range of knowledge, and a special kind of *overview*, to the solution of such problems.

And it was just that overview, Talis said, that gave them an early warning of a new problem within the human worlds. A threat, a danger, that might well in the end affect the future of the entire galaxy.

Keill might have interrupted again, but the old man, not to be hurried, held up a hand to stop him.

'When we saw the magnitude of this danger,' Talis continued, 'we made up our minds that we must pool all our resources, all our knowledge and abilities, to oppose it. We also knew that if we opposed it, we ourselves would be in immediate danger. So we abandoned the lives we were then leading, and came here.'

'Where is *here* ?' Keill asked.

'We are on – more correctly, within – an asteroid,' Talis said. 'A wandering piece of space debris, which appears on no star maps or charts of the spaceways.'

And he explained how he and the nameless others had constructed a secret base for themselves within the asteroid – with the most advanced laboratories, communications equipment and special protective devices that they could contrive. It had been a long, slow process, for secrecy had to be absolute. During the process, Talis said, all of his companions had disappeared from their home worlds, as undramatically as possible. They had made sure that official records would show, if anyone inquired, that many of them had died, as old people will. The rest of them would have seemed to have retired, fading away into obscurity and senility.

'We know that we cannot be traced here, or located,' Talis said. 'And we know that here we must stay, within our asteroid, and do everything in our power to counter the growing threat – that may one day soon endanger the very existence of the galaxy as we know it.'

Keill frowned dubiously. 'You'll pardon me if I find all this hard to take in. What is this terrible threat? And what is it all to do with me being here?'

'Do not take it too lightly, Keill Randor.' The old voice was sombre. 'We are confronting an enemy of frightening power, and even more frightening intentions. He is all humanity's enemy – but he is even more particularly your enemy. For he is the one who murdered your world.'

chapter six

Shock jolted Keill into a sitting position – but the movement drenched him with sweat again, and dizziness swept over him, blurring his vision. He sagged back against the cushioned bed, and the hooded figure in the holo-image leaned forward anxiously.

'You must not over-tax yourself,' Talis said. 'I have spoken for too long, and I fear I have distressed you. Now you must rest, and we will speak again when you are stronger.'

'No – wait . . .' Keill said weakly. 'I must know . . .'

But the holo-image vanished as abruptly as it had appeared, and the room was silent once more.

Keill lay back, limp with the emotions that boiled within him, the desperate need to know more. He might have tried to shout, even to get up, though his limbs felt as if they were made of water. But a sound from one side diverted him.

Twisting his head around, he saw a section of the wall swing silently inwards, though there had been no sign of a door-seam. Through the opening rolled a wheeled, upright cylindrical shape – a robot servitor, bearing a beaker upon its level upper surface.

It came to a stop beside the bed. The beaker held a milky liquid, fragrant, steaming slightly. Keill found that he was desperately thirsty. He picked up the beaker, grimly forbidding his hand to shake, and drained the contents. When the empty beaker was replaced, the servitor rolled away, and the wall closed as blank and seamless as before.

The drink had been bland, but flavoursome and warm. It also seemed soothing, relaxing – and then Keill knew that it was certainly drugged, that again the numbness was invading his mind, quietening its turmoil, and he was drifting into sleep.

When he awoke again he felt as refreshed as before, and more of his strength seemed to have returned. He was able to sit up without effort – though when he swung his legs off the bed and tried to stand, he found himself shaky, and was glad to sink back down on to the contoured padding.

But the room remained empty. Keill tried shouting, calling Talis's name, demanding his return – but no image formed, no voice came.

Instead the robot servitor appeared, as before. It bore another drink – a clear, cool liquid this time – and a bowl containing a gruel-like substance. Keill tasted them suspiciously at first, but growing thirst and hunger drove him to empty the containers. And this time there was no drug, only refreshment, pleasant tastes, and the restorative feeling of food in the stomach.

The robot's entrance had also coincided with the opening of another panel in the wall behind Keill, revealing a small shower-and-lavatory unit, as compact as the same facility on a spaceship. He needed the support of the robot to make use of it, and fell back exhausted when he returned to the bed. But it was another step ahead, another step towards the time when his strength would be returned and he could become his own master again – and begin to find out what was really happening.

From then on, the undisturbed days continued – if they were days, for Keill had no way of measuring the passage of time within the blank-walled room. He slept and woke, ate and drank, rested and thought – sorting through the questions and the doubts that swarmed within him.

He could not bring himself to accept what he had been told by the old man called Talis – because it seemed too improbable, and because too much had been left unexplained. A group

58

of aged scientists hiding themselves away so as to fight some nameless enemy? The same enemy being the destroyer who had wiped out the Legions of Moros?

The questions of 'who' and 'why' bulked too large, too unanswerable. And he had been offered no evidence of any of it, save one holo-image of an old man keeping his face hidden.

He assembled what facts he had, testing their solidity. He had just entered his ship, on Saltrenius, when someone – or something – had come behind him and felled him with a needler. He was now in an empty room somewhere, tended by a robot. He had gone through some prolonged physical ordeal, which had left him weakened – and which had seemed to require some highly sophisticated technology. And he was free of pain.

Or was he? Was even that a true fact? Certainly there were drugs that could blot out even that much pain. But he did not feel drugged – he was alert and clear-headed, despite his body's shakiness.

Then perhaps, as he had thought before, he was lying in a hospital somewhere, in the terminal stages of his illness, finishing out his life in delirium.

Did the hallucinations of delirium go on as long as these past events seemed to have? He did not know. Would they be so detailed, in such an ordered routine, as his days now were in this room? He did not know.

The questions pursued themselves round in circles within his mind till he was weary of them. In the end, he knew very little. In time, perhaps, if Talis returned, or if other developments came along, he would learn more.

Meanwhile, his legionary discipline reasserted itself. A man did not fret over situations he could not hope to alter. A man did not waste energy gnawing at questions for which there seemed, as yet, no answers. If it was necessary to wait, then a man must wait – calm, controlled, patient.

And he must keep himself ready at all times to act, instantly, when action became possible.

So Keill readied himself. He began a programme of light exercises at regular intervals – routine ones that he had known from childhood. As he grew stronger, he extended the workouts, regaining more and more of his normal suppleness, agility and strength. And he was aware that Talis, or someone, was keeping his progress under observation – for his meals grew larger and more substantial as his output of energy increased.

Then one day, as if to underline how far he had come from being weak and bed-ridden, the robot brought not only his usual meal but also his clothing.

His full uniform was there – cleaned, fresh, showing no signs of wear. As if it were a new one made exactly to the specifications of the old.

He dressed quickly, delighting in the familiarity of the garments, feeling even more fully himself. And his delight increased when he slipped a hand into a tunic pocket and drew out the light chain with, dangling from it, his identity disc. Its angry red glow faded, shifted to the sky-blue of normality as he took it in his hand, then quickly put the chain round his neck.

Now, he thought, I am a legionary again.

Even so, the routine went on, and still no contact came from Talis. Keill persisted in his self-directed programme of exercise, testing himself ever more strenuously. Until the time came at last when he could put himself through the complete routine of gruelling physical stresses that had formed his basic training scheme for the Festival of Martial Games, on Moros.

When he emerged from that routine sweating only lightly, his breathing even, his body still resilient, with a reserve of energy left, he knew he was ready.

The time of waiting was over.

When the robot next came, Keill did not hesitate. As the wall panel swung open, he simply hurdled the small wheeled cylinder, and was out – to seek his freedom.

*

He found himself in a narrow passageway, dimly lit, with metallic floor, walls and ceiling. Closed doors, like the hatchways of spaceships, interrupted the smoothness of one wall here and there along its length.

The doors were tightly secured, and Keill did not waste energy trying to break through them. They were made of the special quaternium alloy used for the hulls of fighting ships, well able to resist heavier assaults than even he could manage bare-handed.

He raced along the passage. It took an L-turn to the right, and offered him two gangways, downwards and upwards. Without pausing he chose the downward steps – and came to a sizeable chamber containing an array of complex machinery, in separated compartments.

Most of this equipment he recognized – the air and water recyclers especially. It all seemed to be larger and more intricate forms of the standard life-support systems for spacecraft. And the bulkiest device, in the central position, was surely a very advanced form of gravitational unit.

So he *was* on some form of space station or artificial satellite, he realized. Perhaps Talis's story of a secret, hollowed-out asteroid was true.

But he would not know unless he could get outside it. And for that he would need at least a space suit, preferably with a weapon, and – if luck were really with him – a ship of some sort.

He retraced his steps, racing up to the upper level. More passageways, but often now with doors that opened. They revealed a series of chambers that were clearly laboratories – crammed, one and all, with collections of equipment that Keill, who thought of himself as fairly knowledgeable about technology, could not begin to fathom.

Another gangway led upwards, and he sprinted along it. It took him up to a chamber heaped, floor to ceiling, with book tapes and information tapes of every kind, and a number of viewers scattered among them. Beyond that room was an observation chamber, with a broad viewscreen offering a pano-ramic segment of star-filled space. Abundant star-maps, charts of the space lanes, computer outlets were available around the room.

It was a welcome sight, for Keill knew that if he was able to escape, he might need the information within that room to get his bearings, and his direction.

But he did not linger there just yet. He had heard no sound of an alarm being raised, nor had there been any sign of pur-suit. But he did not doubt that his disappearance from the room had been noted – and Talis, or someone, would surely be working out how to put an end to his wild flight.

Another passageway, and more closed doors. Another gangway, leading again to a higher level. Another chamber . . .

He came to an abrupt halt, barely able to contain the yell of exultation that rose in his chest.

The broad chamber before him – with a high, curved ceiling that had to be the outer hull of whatever space structure he was in – contained his own ship.

It gleamed and shone as it had not done since it had first come out of production on Moros. Old battle scars and stains had been removed, the blue Legion insignia re-embossed, the blunt snouts of the weapons polished. It looked as newly re-made as his uniform had. And it was the most heartening sight Keill had seen for a long time.

His first instinct was simply to climb in and blast his way out through the ceiling. But as he began to move round the ship towards the entrance, he hesitated.

It might be more sensible, he thought, to arm himself from the store of weapons in his ship, and go in search of Talis. Even if he had to burn his way through some of those closed doors.

Then he would be able to demand answers to all those cru-cial questions that the old man had left hanging in the air. About why he was keeping Keill there. And what Talis knew of the destruction of Moros.

It was possible that his store of weapons had been removed from the ship. But at least the airlock hatch was invitingly open, the ramp down. And there was no one in the way.

But as he approached the ramp, he heard a weirdly out-of-place sound. One he had heard before – the night he had tried to steal his own ship, on Saltrenius.

Like a cloth, flapping in the wind . . .

He glanced up, and froze.

A winged creature, like nothing he had ever seen, was hovering above his ship.

The wings – broad, veined membranes that looked flimsy, almost translucent – flapped again as the creature settled upon the ship's hatchway. There it perched, folding its wings, re-garding Keill through two large, colourless, perfectly circular eyes.

Its body was less than a metre high, and narrow, covered with what looked like overlapping plates of soft skin, purplish-grey. Its head seemed too large for the little body, rounded and dome-like, with a small tapering snout beneath the great eyes. And it was a biped – though each of the two small feet seemed in fact more like hands, having three sturdy, jointed toes like fingers, and a fourth one opposing, like a thumb.

But it was not perched on both feet. It was balanced on one.

The other one was, incredibly, gripping a needle-gun – and aiming it unwaveringly at Keill.

Keill's astonishment deepened even further in the next instant – when he heard a voice.

Not the voice, as before, of the old man called Talis. Not any kind of voice that Keill could hear externally, in his ears.

This voice formed itself within Keill's mind.

And it said:

Is it not comical, human-called-Randor, that I must once again use a weapon to keep you from your own ship?

chapter seven

At gun-point, with the winged creature fluttering behind and above him – out of reach even if Keill had been tempted to attack it – he was herded out of the domed chamber that held his spaceship. Down another passage they went, the creature's wing-tips brushing the walls, and finally through a door that, Keill remembered, had been solidly locked when he had come that way before.

Now it swung silently open, revealing a long, low, abundantly furnished room that was clearly designed for comfort and relaxation. Low, cushioned seats were scattered around on the soft floor-covering, the lighting was quiet and mellow, tables here and there were piled with book tapes.

Keill took it all in with a glance, reserving his full attention for the figure seated in the centre of the room. It was Talis, robed and cowled as before – but there was no doubt that this time it was not a holo-image. He was there in the flesh.

The old man gestured towards a chair opposite him, inviting Keill to sit. Keill did so slowly, turning to watch the winged creature – which settled on the back of another chair, folding its delicate wings, still well out of reach. And still aiming the needle-gun at Keill, while gazing at him unblinkingly with its round, luminous eyes.

'I very much regret . . .' Talis's kindly voice began.

Keill interrupted. 'Is this,' he asked, gesturing at the creature, 'the thing that attacked me on Saltrenius?'

Talis sighed. 'Yes, but attacked is not really the right word . . .'

'What is it?' Keill demanded.

'An alien,' said Talis, 'of a race that calls itself the Ehrlil. From another galaxy.'

Keill was startled, but his face remained impassive. 'And telepathic?'

Before Talis could reply, words again formed soundlessly in the depths of Keill's mind.

I project with ease, human. But I receive with difficulty from the mudheads of this galaxy.

Keill frowned, feeling slightly unnerved. 'I think, old man, that you are setting up some kind of elaborate hoax, for reasons that I cannot guess.'

'It is no hoax,' Talis said quietly. 'I have told you only the truth.'

'But an alien? A mind-reading alien?'

It was not impossible, Keill knew. Just highly unlikely. Intergalactic travel had been tried many times by human explorers – but it presented its own special problems and rigours, and few had returned. Those that did come back had mostly had their minds unhinged by loneliness, unknown dangers and the long-term effects of Overlight, and their babbled accounts made little sense. But recent history included some tales of alien beings making the intergalactic journey in the other direction – and making brief, uneventful contact with humans on the Inhabited Worlds, before going on their unguessable ways.

Keill had never seen such an alien, though, nor had he ever met anyone who had.

Yet there were no such beings native to his own galaxy. When man first went out among the stars, during the Scattering, the planets that were to become the Inhabited Worlds held many kinds of strange life forms. But it had been a grave disappointment for the early colonists (though, for some, a relief) that none of the life forms had been intelligent. Mankind found himself to be the only intelligent species in his galaxy.

As for telepathy, again Keill knew that it probably existed

in some form. He had heard of a few humans – some of the altered ones, whose planets had produced mutations in their human populations – who could reach into other minds. But always in a limited, erratic way.

He brought his attention back to Talis, who was expounding on the subject. '. . . an intrepid race of explorers, it seems, who think nothing of the awesome emptiness between galaxies. They are very long-lived, of course, and are always in mental contact with one another . . .'

'Why is it here?' Keill demanded.

'Not *it*,' Talis said with a chuckle, '*she*. Glr is a female of her species.'

'All right,' Keill said patiently, 'why is *she* here?'

'Her ship developed a malfunction,' Talis replied, 'and she was forced to land on a human world. In time a leading scientist met her and befriended her. And she has stayed, finding humanity a source of considerable interest . . .'

And amusement, said the voice in Keill's mind, with soundless laughter behind it.

'When we began the process of setting up our base,' Talis went on, 'Glr came as well.'

'I find this no easier to believe than anything else you tell me,' Keill said gruffly. 'Surely the arrival of such an alien would have been widely reported throughout the Worlds. But I have heard nothing of this . . . Glr.'

'I told you the Ehrlil are long-lived,' said Talis. 'Her arrival was reported – but it was some sixty years ago. The scientist who befriended her was my father.'

Keill leaned back against the cushions of his chair, feeling slightly dazed. And the alien's voice formed in his mind again, still bubbling with laughter.

I am in fact quite young – about four of your centuries. The Ehrlil elders think of me as a wayward, foolish child whose curiosity will get her into trouble.

*

Keill shook his head as if to clear it. Again he wondered if he was in the grip of some nightmare from a terminal delirium – or if Talis was merely a crazed old space hermit with an odd taste in pets. Pets with guns.

'Isn't it time,' he said at last, 'that you told me what I'm doing here, being held at gunpoint by an alien?'

'I regret the gun,' Talis said quickly. 'But the others felt that, because you are given to rash and hasty action, I ought not meet you in person without some protection.'

'Fearing I might attack you?' Keill said. 'If I wanted to do so, old man, your flying alien would not stop me.' Behind him the creature's wings flared, but he ignored it. 'And I might do so yet – if you don't start *now* to give me some explanations.'

'Of course,' Talis said soothingly. 'That is why we are here. But there is so much to tell . . .'

'I know,' Keill said, 'and so much you can't tell me. You said as much, earlier. But you *will* tell me, old man. You'll tell me why I am here – and what you know about this person, this enemy, who you say destroyed Moros.'

'The enemy,' Talis replied sombrely, 'is why you are here. Just as he is why my group and myself are here.'

'So you also have said,' Keill interrupted. 'But I have seen only yourself, and your alien.'

'The others are nearby, and are listening. You may see them if you wish – though I fear you will learn little from it.'

He moved one hand to the side of his chair, and a portion of the wall nearest them grew hazy – changing, as Keill watched, from a solid surface into what seemed to be a window, but was in fact an enlarged viewscreen.

It revealed a group of people, sitting quietly together. Like Talis, most of them seemed elderly – as far as Keill could tell. For, also like Talis, each of them wore a voluminous robe, with a cowl that kept the face in darkness.

Keill smiled sardonically. 'More mystery. What do you call yourselves – the Hooded Brethren of Secrecy?'

68

Talis moved his hand again, and the silent group faded from view, the wall resuming its smooth solidity. 'You will come to understand our need for secrecy,' he said quietly. 'And we have no name for ourselves – though Glr has given us one.'

I call them the 'Overseers', said the alien's voice in Keill's mind, *because they alone among you mudheads seem able to see the wholeness of events in this galaxy. You would do well, Randor, to show them some respect.*

'I will show respect,' Keill replied aloud, 'when I have been given proof that respect is due.'

'Just so,' said Talis. 'I wish to provide such proof. I want you to understand what we began to see, more than two years ago.'

The group, Talis went on, made regular, wide-ranging studies of major happenings in the Inhabited Worlds. They analysed and investigated, and often they also made projections – trying to foresee problems before they occurred, so they could aid and advise planetary leaders whose worlds might be affected.

In the course of their work, they began to see a strange and unsettling pattern in many of the events – no matter how widely scattered these events might be in the Galaxy. They made more studies, more analyses – and reached their conclusion.

'The fact was inescapable,' Talis said. 'It was that many more *wars* were happening, everywhere, than should have been happening.'

Keill frowned. 'There are always wars.'

'Of course. But mostly local wars, growing out of local conditions – and happening at random, with no connections among them.' The old man leaned forward intently. 'But the wars we studied had too much in common, for mere coincidence. Too much of a pattern.'

What a violent species you are, said the amused alien voice.

Talis went on, unaware of the interruption. 'I will give you tapes to study, which are summaries of our findings. You will see for yourself that the pattern had to be *contrived*. Someone was setting out with the conscious, murderous intention of *starting* wars, around the galaxy.'

'And this someone is the enemy you speak of?'

'Just so.'

'Who is he? And where?'

Talis sighed. 'That I cannot tell you, because we do not yet know. We know only that such a being must exist. We know his ruthless and evil purpose, and we know something of his methods. No more. Except that for convenience we have given him something of a code name. We call him the Warlord.'

Keill's frown deepened. 'You'll show me evidence that this . . . Warlord . . . exists?'

'We will. But you already possess one proof of his reality.'

Keill tensed, suspecting what was coming. 'What proof?'

'The murder of the Legions.'

'Go on,' Keill said fiercely.

'Consider,' Talis said. 'Everyone knew the reputation of the Legions – that they would fight only on the side of people who were defending themselves, whose cause contained some right and justice in it. But words like right and justice are not in the vocabulary of the Warlord. He would surely have foreseen a time when a war he sought might be prevented by the Legions. And he might have foreseen a time when the Legions themselves would guess at his existence, and move against him directly. It may be that your Central Command had already guessed. So – he moved first, with power we had not imagined, to erase that threat.'

'A pre-emptive strike,' Keill said through gritted teeth.

'Just so.'

'If any of this is true,' Keill said bitterly, 'such a war-maker would have to be insane.'

'It is all true,' Talis replied, 'and he may well be insane – with the kind of madness that keeps company with a hunger

70

for ultimate power. For we believe it is his aim to set the Inhabited Worlds at each other's throats, in war upon war that gradually spread to more and more planets – ultimately to the entire galaxy. And out of that evil, that terrible destruction, he would hope to emerge as the sole and supreme ruler over what remains of all humanity.'

chapter eight

The information tapes provided by Talis, summarizing long months of investigation by the Overseers, were voluminous and thorough. Hour upon hour Keill sat at the viewer, his patient concentration never wavering – hardly aware of consuming the food and drink brought to him at one point by the robot servitor.

He saw, on the tapes, human societies upon world after world torn apart by war. On one distant planet, far-flung tribes of nomads who had roamed their grasslands for peaceful generations came together, over a few brief years, for no understandable reason, to launch a vicious attack on the scattered cities of that planet. On another world, where the people of its one populated continent lived in wealth and plenty because of their supplies of a valuable mineral, a ferocious civil war broke out between two political groups – each side wrongly believing that the other was seeking total control over the mineral.

He saw entire solar systems erupt with violence. In one, a large, industrialized planet moved suddenly and inexplicably to attack a smaller, under-developed neighbour. Elsewhere, two small planets came together to invade – without clear cause – a third, and then after their victory fell out and fought between themselves.

He saw such wars arise, time and again, without warning and almost without reason. An irrational growth of racial prejudice between two planets that had once been wholly friendly – an eruption of a new religious cult that led its followers into holy war – an unexplained political assassination – an outburst of space piracy – a senseless breakdown of simple trade negotiations . . .

And much more. As the hours passed and the facts accumulated, the tapes made the crucial points clear. In each case there had been no likelihood or prospect of war – until something had begun stirring up the worst elements of the human character. Greed and self-interest; the urge to power; suspicion, prejudice and fear. And these stirrings were fed by unexpected events – and by deception, lying propaganda, treachery and murder.

Further, Keill saw, on every one of the planets there were one or two people who had seemed to come out of nowhere, but who rose swiftly to positions of power and influence. These individuals were always at the heart of the events that led to the catastrophe of war.

Finally, his mind swimming with the terrible images that had been revealed to him, Keill returned to the relaxation room in search of Talis. The old man had preceded him, and was waiting, still shadowed within his cowl.

'Now you have seen the summaries of our findings,' the old voice said, 'do you believe what I have told you?'

Keill looked at him impassively for a long moment. 'I have seen the stories of a great many wars,' he said at last. 'None of them pleasant – but wars never are.'

'Did you not perceive the pattern?' Talis insisted.

Keill shrugged. 'I saw resemblances. But the essence of war is usually much the same, wherever it happens. I saw no final proof of *connections*. And I still find it hard to believe that all those wars were caused by one . . . Warlord. Surely others would have guessed at the existence of such a being.'

'The galaxy is large,' Talis said, 'and there is not enough information-sharing among planets. Aside from trade and short-range travelling, there are hardly any galaxy-wide links.

74

So no one would assemble all the data, to see what is happening on the overall, galactic scale.'

'Except yourselves.'

'Just so.'

'Yet for all your *overview*,' Keill said bluntly, 'you seem to know very little. What of these individuals that the tapes singled out – the ones who rose so quickly to positions of power?'

'They are of course servants of the Warlord,' Talis replied, 'sent as emissaries to worm their way into positions where they can spread the infection that leads to war.'

'Could you not have these people investigated,' Keill asked, 'to see if there are connections among them that might lead back to your Warlord?'

'It has been tried,' said Talis glumly. 'But on most worlds where they have appeared, they have quickly become too powerful to be investigated. In the few cases, though, where a planet has resisted the infection, and has stopped the Warlord's servants before they gained power, we have learned some things. We have learned that the Warlord is hidden even to his emissaries, who receive their orders indirectly. And we have learned that a *failed* emissary, like those of whom I speak, does not remain alive for long.'

'It is not much,' Keill said.

'True – but we dare not press too hard. As far as we know the Warlord has not guessed our existence. And he must not, as yet, for we know too little to oppose him properly. That is why we, too, are so secretive – even with you, Keill Randor. If you were ever to fall into the hands of the Warlord or his servants, they would not be able to wrest knowledge from you that you do not have – of who we are, where we are.'

Keill smiled dryly. 'You must hide, so he won't know of you – yet while you're hiding, you can't learn more of him. This is foolishness!'

'No,' said Talis quietly, 'it is the reason why we, too, need an emissary.'

'By which,' Keill said, 'you mean me.'

'Just so. We cannot go out among the Worlds ourselves. We have devices that can monitor events on nearly any planet of our choosing – but we need someone to be our eyes and ears at close range. Someone who can go on to worlds threatened by the Warlord – and survive.'

'One man against this . . . emperor of wars?'

'Not just a man. A legionary. No one in the galaxy would have a higher potential for survival.'

But as Talis spoke, another voice was also speaking – in Keill's mind.

In the midst of all your doubts, Randor, you would do well to remember that you survive now only because of the Overseers' skills, which they gave to you at considerable risk.

Keill turned swiftly. The alien, Glr, was floating across the room on her translucent wings, to settle on a perch near the door, her great eyes fixed as before on Keill.

'I haven't forgotten,' he said slowly, 'the unpayable debt I owe, for my healing. If I *am* healed.'

Glr fluttered her wings as if echoing the exasperation in Talis's voice. 'Do you doubt even that?'

'The medic told me,' Keill said stubbornly, 'that the effects of the radiation couldn't be reversed.'

'True,' Talis replied. 'It had settled in your bones, irreversibly. So – we replaced them.'

'Replaced . . . ?'

'A process of my own invention, if I may say so,' Talis went on. 'Your skeletal structure is now composed of an organic alloy.'

Keill stared at him speechlessly.

'It was an interesting operation. The replacement had to be done molecule by molecule, taking care to match your original skeleton exactly in shape and weight, and to ensure that your bone marrow adapted. But—' he gestured expansively at Keill —'it all seems entirely successful.'

Keill did not see the gesture. He was looking down at himself, at his arms and legs, his ribs, his knuckles . . .

'There is an interesting side effect,' Talis continued chattily. 'The alloy has quite surprising resilience and strength. Our tests have shown that it is almost completely infrangible.'

'Infrangible? What . . .'

It means, mudhead, laughed Glr in his mind, *that your bones cannot be broken.*

Keill's head jerked up, eyes wide with disbelief. Then a smile began to form on his lips – a smile of scornful irony, but tinged with disappointment.

'Now you have gone too far,' he said. 'If you thought you could ease my doubts with a wild tale like that . . .'

I would gladly arrange a test for you, Glr put in, *but your flesh would suffer painful bruising in the process.*

Keill stood up abruptly. 'Talis, if that is your name, I can swallow no more absurdity. You may cling to your fantasies of Warlords and galactic empires – and bone replacements – and tell them to the next fool who comes along. But I have something else to do – a task put on me by a dear friend who tried to save me while she herself was dying. I'm going to look for the one who destroyed Moros, whoever it may be, if it takes the rest of my life, long or short. And I'm going to start looking on that moon of Saltrenius – with no more delay.'

He turned and moved to the door. But the alien was there before him – wings spread, sturdy fingers revealing small, sharp talons, equally sharp little teeth gleaming in the narrow mouth.

Keill halted. 'Old man, I wish no harm to you or to this creature. But I'm leaving, one way or another.'

Talis raised a hand, and some mental message must have passed between him and Glr, for the alien swirled away from the door and settled.

'I would not stop you leaving, Keill Randor,' said the old man. 'I have told you all I can tell you – I cannot force you to believe me. But certainly, the moon called Creffa is exactly where we *wish* you to go.'

77

Keill turned back, surprised. 'But before, on Saltrenius . . . You went to some lengths to *stop* me.'

'Of course. You were dying then – and you were going into danger unprepared.' The old hand moved as before, to the side of the chair. 'Bear with me a moment longer, and observe.'

Again the surface of the nearby wall shivered. But this time it was not the silent group of hooded figures that Keill saw.

Instead the screen revealed an eerie alien landscape, stark, rock-strewn, the shadows deep black and sharply defined. In the background rose the high, curved surface of a life-support dome, sleek and shiny in the brilliant light.

In the foreground was the bulky, cylindrical shape of a spaceship – which Keill recognized at once.

The cruiser he had seen at the Saltrenius spaceport. The ship that belonged to the three men who called themselves legionaries.

'This is Creffa,' Talis said. 'I see you have recognized the ship. One of our monitoring devices recorded this scene within the last few days.'

Keill said nothing, but watched. The airlock of the ship was opening, and figures were appearing.

They were spacesuited, of course, but Keill did not need to see faces to the first man who descended to the dusty surface. A head taller than the others, enormous width of shoulder . . . The mocking giant who preferred to wear only half a legionary uniform.

Behind him from the ship, stooping under sizeable containers of what must have been supplies, came other figures. Not just the two that Keill had expected. The giant had acquired some new companions.

In all, there were nine men who left the ship and made their way, through the light gravity of Creffa, towards the dome.

'Are there more inside?' Keill asked, as the image faded from the screen.

'No,' Talis said. 'Only the nine. Six more had been recruited – from the criminal element on Saltrenius – before we took you

78

from the planet. And hear me, Keill Randor – not one of them is a legionary.'

Keill nodded. 'As I thought. I was certain before that the first three were not.'

Surprise showed in Talis's voice. 'You knew? Yet you were going – ill as you were, and unaided – to walk into their trap?'

'A trap is no trap if it is expected,' Keill said. 'I had to go. As I still must – whether there are nine or ninety.'

'Just so,' Talis replied. 'Much could be learned, many questions answered, by patient and careful observation on Creffa.'

'Observation?' Keill echoed with a grim smile. 'Something more, Talis. It's clear that whoever destroyed Moros also sent those men to pose as legionaries, and to set up a base that would attract any survivors. I want to spring that trap before any real legionaries walk into it unknowingly.' His voice grew tense. 'Some may already have done so while I've been here.'

The cowled figure shook his head. 'None has. Our monitoring devices have kept a full-time watch. In the same way, all our devices have searched and scoured the galaxy, since the day of Moros's destruction, looking for surviving legionaries. We have found none – except yourself.'

Keill was stunned, hearing the words he had been half-dreading for so long. 'There must be some! You can't monitor the entire galaxy!'

'If there are,' Talis said softly, 'they are in hiding. They are not moving around the galaxy as you did, searching for their fellows. Had any done so, we would have located them – just as we located you.' He reached a sympathetic hand towards Keill. 'No, I greatly fear . . . that you may be the last legionary.'

Keill's face revealed little of the torment within him – only a momentary twisting of his features, a flash of anguish in his eyes. Then his control returned, and he gazed calmly at Talis.

'Even if that is true,' he said levelly, 'I am still going to this moon, to do what must be done.'

Well spoken, said the bright inner voice of Glr. *Foolish, stubborn and brave – no wonder humans are so short-lived.*

79

Keill ignored the interruption, for Talis had raised an admonishing hand. 'I agree, you must go. But I urge you – do not plunge into rash action. Use caution!'

Keill rose to his feet, smiling thinly. 'Talis, it is too late for caution. A time always comes when it is necessary to *act*, not merely to observe. That time has come now, for me – and for those impostors on Creffa.'

part three
Killers' moon

chapter nine

Enveloped in the misted nothingness of Overlight, Keill Randor completed his routine check of his spaceship's systems, leaned back in the slingseat and stretched luxuriously.

He was relaxed, entirely at ease, and glad to be on the move. Inaction was nearly the worst torment of all, he thought. Especially when inaction had been forced on him, by the old man on the hidden asteroid. So much time had been lost, while he had lain unconscious, and then while he had slowly recovered, after . . . whatever had been done to him. Time that the false legionaries, in their base on the moon called Creffa, would have used to strengthen their position.

But at least they were still there, according to the Overseers' monitoring devices. And no legionaries had walked into that trap . . .

Keill pushed that thought away. He was not willing to face the possible truth of old Talis's statement that there *were* no other legionaries. He was not sure that he could ever face the possibility that he might be the last of his race – which meant living with a unique and terrible loneliness for the rest of his life.

Again he brought his thoughts under control. Loneliness of any kind was not a subject to dwell on in deep space, especially not in the emptiness of Overlight. It could do strange things to a human mind, if that mind turned to brooding and fretting. The best remedy was keeping busy.

He glanced down again at the last read-out, still showing on his computer screen from his systems check. The Overseers had certainly renewed his ship, but had sensibly left its components as they were, as Keill was used to. He knew that they could easily have built in some wonderfully advanced technology, superior to the systems in his ship – but he would have needed more time to be trained to use it. They may well have made some slight adjustments to the ship's computer guidance systems, but that did not affect Keill. The ship remained as familiar as ever, like an extension of his own body and reflexes.

He thought back to his departure from the asteroid – if it was an asteroid. As mysterious and secretive as ever, Talis had instructed Keill to keep his viewscreens blank after he entered his ship, and to keep them that way until he entered Overlight. His ship computer had been preprogrammed, Talis had said, to take the ship off the asteroid and then to enter Overlight as soon as possible.

And, Talis had added, the computer had been programmed to erase those instructions once Keill was in Overlight.

Keill had wondered about that statement. If the Overseers had intended him to go out as their emissary, as Talis had said earlier, how would he ever have contacted them, reported to them? Talis had read his puzzlement correctly, and had explained.

'If you ever have any wish to contact us,' the old man had said, 'we have provided a communications link. It will be there when you need it.'

At the time, with his doubts and disbeliefs still strong, Keill had not given much thought to the statement. He had felt that there was never likely to be a time when he would want to make any contact with the old man and his peculiar, hooded friends. But now, out in space, that vague assurance of a communications link worried him.

Communications were definitely one of the Overseers' specialities. He had been shown some of their monitoring devices, of the sort that they had scattered around the Inhabited Worlds – amazingly intricate but compact objects, some no bigger than a fist, none larger than a man's head. Operating like spy satellites, they could pick up, record and transmit most forms of broadcast media from a planet's surface, whether electronic, holo or whatever. They could also, from orbit, film and transmit visual images of a planet that were astonishingly detailed – as Keill had seen with the tape of the nine men on Creffa. And the devices were nearly undetectable by the people of any planet, because of their size and the erratic orbits that were built into them.

Also, if anyone did locate them by accident, the devices would self-destruct before they could be examined closely.

That fact especially troubled Keill.

One of the pleasures of being away from the asteroid had been the feeling of personal freedom – of not being watched. He had known, all the time he was there, that he had been under scrutiny by similar monitors. But was he still being watched? Was there a device hidden on his ship, monitoring him? Or was the communications link that Talis had mentioned merely waiting somewhere in the ship – waiting for the moment when he might need it, before somehow becoming activated?

If so, where was it? And was it, too, programmed to self-destruct if wrongly handled?

He strongly hoped that the Overseers had not planted such a device on the ship. If he came across it unknowingly, and mishandled it, he could blow himself out of the sky.

Time to make a search, he thought.

He unstrapped himself from the slingseat and stood up. The familiar drift of his body, in null-gravity, did not trouble him. The boots of his spacesuit adhered to the treated deck of the ship, keeping him from floating. He moved towards a row of compartments that extended across one side of the single inner chamber of the ship. They held all his necessities – food supplies in one, weapons in another, clothing and personal possessions in another, and so on.

One thing about a single-person fighter, he thought, there are only so many places where an object can be hidden. Besides those compartments, there were the ship's various systems – the drive, life support, ship's weapons and the rest –

behind heavy bulkheads at the nose and stern. He could go through all possible storage spaces in a few minutes. But he would be thorough, he told himself, and take his time. If the Overseers had planted a monitor, it could be extremely miniaturized. But there was time – about half an hour yet before he would come out of Overlight near the planet Saltrenius.

And then something odd happened, something totally irrational.

He began to laugh.

Not out loud, but to himself, within himself. Carefree, bubbling laughter . . .

No, he thought – and anger surged up in him, blotting out the laughter. It's not me. It's that alien – that winged, telepathic giggler of an alien.

Instantly the silent, laughing voice formed in his mind. *Now that you have discovered me, may I be released? Your weapons store does not suit my dignity.*

Keill moved swiftly to the weapons compartment and flung open its door.

The round, colourless eyes of the little alien gazed at him, unblinkingly.

Your communications link reporting for duty, sir, it said.

The alien floated out, automatically spreading its wings despite the null-gravity, and drifted over to the control panel. There it settled on the edge, gripping with the strange little feet that were like hands. And Keill followed, speechless with anger, flinging himself into the slingseat, glaring at the creature. It returned his look calmly, but the silent laughter faded.

I warned Talis you would be angry, the inner voice said. *But he felt you would not allow me to accompany you if you knew beforehand.*

'He was quite right,' said Keill coldly. 'And I don't want you to accompany me now. Give me the figures, and I'll alter course and take you back.'

I cannot, the alien said. *I do not know the coordinates.*

86

'You must!' Keill said. 'Surely even those senile old mad-men wouldn't send you away unless you could get back!'

I can get back, the voice replied. *But I do not know how.*

As Keill was about to explode, the alien hastily went on: *The data is in my unconscious memory. Talis can recall me by projecting a certain code to my mind. I will then automatically programme the computer for return. But I will at once forget the data, consciously – just as the computer will erase the figures from its memory once the new course is begun.*

Again Keill was speechless. More of Talis's cursed secrecy. And, like every action of the Overseers, it seemed both so plausible – and yet so wholly mad.

Then a thought struck him. 'You can reach Talis's mind from here?'

The reach of an Ehrlil mind has no limits in space. The little alien spoke matter-of-factly, without pride.

'If so,' Keill said, 'you could have remained on the asteroid, and still set up a "communications link" with me, wherever I was.'

True.

'Then why are you here?' Keill shouted.

Talis did not wish you to go into danger unaided.

'Unaided?' Keill echoed. 'I'm to face nine men who will almost certainly try to kill me – and I must do so with you filling my mind with crazed giggling?'

I will not get in your way. The alien's silent voice seemed hurt. *But I can use a weapon, as you know. And pilot your ship.*

'You can pilot this ship?'

Human ships are child's play – even for a child like myself. The words held a trace of laughter, quickly fading. *How do you think you were taken from Saltrenius to the asteroid?*

Keill pondered. 'Perhaps then you can be of use.'

He had worried, earlier, about leaving his craft unattended after landing on Creffa. If some of his enemies located it, he would have his escape cut off. But now, with the alien . . .

Exactly, the inner voice said, replying to his thought. *I will guard your ship. And whatever else you wish. I am under your orders.*

'All right,' Keill said at last. 'As long as you remember that, and don't start taking orders from Talis at long range. Remember that I'm going on a task of my own choosing. I'm not the Overseers' emissary – and I want no interference, from them or from you.'

It will be as you say. The thought seemed saddened. *But you are being needlessly stubborn. All that Talis told you is the truth.*

Keill was disturbed by the words, and by the clear sincerity and earnestness behind them. Such things could not be pretended, in a telepathic voice.

'No doubt you believe it,' Keill said. 'But I'm not concerned now with tales of Warlords and the rest of it. My concern is with nine men on Creffa, and what I can get out of them about the death of my world.'

It is all the same thing, said the alien patiently. *Can you not see that the death of Moros should demand your belief in the Warlord? Such an act could only be done by someone extremely powerful, and extremely ruthless.*

Keill did not reply at once. It was a point that he himself always came back to. Who was there in the galaxy dangerous enough, insane enough, to destroy the Legions? How could an attacker get past the defences of Moros? And, most of all, *why*?

When it came down to answers, he thought ruefully, Talis's story of the Warlord was the only one he had been given, by anyone. If only it was not so unlikely . . .

Only your stubbornness makes it so, came the voice of the alien.

'That's another thing,' Keill said sharply. 'While you're here, you will keep out of my mind. My thoughts are my own.'

I told you before that I receive with difficulty from humans, the alien replied. *I could not read the deeper levels of your mind if I wished to. I can receive only those thoughts that you form clearly, on the surface of your mind, as if you were speaking them.*

'Nothing more?' Keill asked suspiciously.

Only blurred impressions, mixtures of emotions. Indeed, that is all I ever get from most humans. You, at least, have some clarity of mind, if not as much as the Overseers. That is one reason why I was willing to come with you.

'One reason?' Keill was interested in spite of himself. 'What are the others?'

First, because I agree with Talis that you will need me, the alien said. *Second, because it is obvious that life in your company will never be unexciting.*

'It might be shorter than you bargained for,' Keill said grimly.

Possibly. But I do not fear dying – except from boredom.

Keill could not help smiling at the words, and a trace of the alien's laughter crept into his mind in response. He leaned back and studied the creature again. The slender, bird-like body, the domed head, the round eyes – it was almost a clownish figure. Yet the brightness of those eyes, and the capability of the hands, belied the foolishness. Keill thought for a moment of this little being, alone in its own ship, penetrating the inconceivable distances from one galaxy to another, facing whatever unknowable dangers lay on such a path . . .

He realized that beyond its appearance, beyond its zany sense of humour, it – no, he corrected himself, *she* – deserved respect. She was a being of high intelligence, ability and courage.

'All right, little friend,' he said at last, still smiling. 'Glr – that is what you are called? We'll be comrades-in-arms, for a while. I hope neither of us will regret it.'

We will not, Keill Randor, said Glr. *For myself, I welcome your friendship. As I will welcome even more the time when you learn that Talis spoke the truth. I hope the knowledge is not acquired too painfully.*

A faint chill prickled Keill's spine. 'Do you read the future, as well as minds?'

No. But I can make predictions, as you can, from the available data.

Before Keill could reply, the computer intruded with a warning tone to draw his attention, and a cluster of figures flashing on to its screen.

They were nearing the point of emerging from Overlight.

Keill turned his concentration to the controls, readying the ship for entrance into normal space, checking the course that would bypass the planet Saltrenius towards a landing on its moon, Creffa.

chapter ten

Creffa was small for a moon, but as airless, rocky, cratered and uninviting as any. Keill's course took him on one orbital sweep, far enough out so that anyone spotting him from the moon's surface would not be able to identify the ship, or imagine that he was anything other than a bypassing ship on its way to planetfall on Saltrenius.

His viewscreens, at extended magnification, showed the gleaming space-dome clearly. The bubble of sturdy metal and plastic was set on a broad, dusty plain on the moon's bright side, yet not far from the sharply defined boundary of the far side's darkness. There were no craters or rock formations within several hundred metres of the dome itself, he saw. A man on foot would have no cover approaching it.

But at least one piece of luck had come his way. The orbital sweep showed that the space cruiser which belonged to the dome's occupants was not in sight.

'Probably on Saltrenius again,' Keill decided.

Some have remained, Glr said. *I can sense human minds within the dome, though I cannot tell how many*.

'Anyway, it lowers the odds,' Keill said. 'And it gives me a chance for some exploring. Whoever's been left in the dome is likely to stay inside.'

He curved his ship to a landing – just inside the deep shadow of the moon's dark side, and over the horizon that would be visible from the dome. He knew that the landing would not be detected: its sound would not travel in the vacuum, and he had chosen a spot surrounded by upthrust clumps of rock that would swallow the vibrations.

Unstrapping himself from the slingseat, he gathered up his

helmet and went to the weapons compartment. It contained a sizeable selection of rifles and pistols, with even a few knives and other hand weapons. But Keill did not hesitate over his choice. He had no illusions about what might happen: if there was a fight, it would be no place for more civilized weapons like anaesthetic needle-guns or stun-guns. Instead he strapped on an ion-energy pistol, a beamer – a modified version of his spaceship's weapons, firing a focused beam of raw energy.

Glr watched the preparations with interest. *You are very calm, for a human*, she said.

'What did you expect?' Keill smiled. 'That my knees would tremble?'

I would have expected some worry or excitement, Glr replied. *It is the human way.*

Keill shrugged his way into his airpack. 'It isn't the Legion way. A waste of energy.'

Some day you must instruct me in the ways of the Legions, Glr said.

Keill laughed. 'Little friend, if I survive this, I'll happily put you through an entire training programme.' He fastened his helmet, swiftly ran through a final check of his equipment, then turned again to Glr, concentrating, trying to form words clearly in his mind, as if speaking them.

'*Are you receiving me?*' he asked.

Perfectly.

'*Good – then we can keep in contact. I want you to stay at the controls, but do absolutely nothing unless I tell you. Clear?*'

Perfectly.

'*And if any of the others spot the ship, and try to board it, let me know at once.*'

I hear and obey. There was a hint of laughter in the reply.

'*Keep your jokes for afterwards. And one more thing – if I don't come back . . .*'

You will be dead, Glr replied calmly, *and no longer able to give me orders. So I will use my initiative.*

Keill smiled. '*All right. Then you can go off and report to your Overseers.*'

I will, said Glr. *But first I might try out the weapons of this ship. On the dome and its occupants.*

The airlock closed silently behind him as Keill dropped to the surface of Creffa. It was a slow, dreamy drop, in the light gravity of the moon – and his progress was also like a dream, long, reaching strides that were in fact huge, slow leaps of many metres at a time. Soon he had reached the edge of the undiffused glare that was the bright side of the moon.

The plastiglass of his helmet darkened instantly, protectively, as he moved across into the light. Behind him, his ship could no longer be seen over the horizon. Ahead, somewhere beyond the jagged clusters of rocks where he stood, the dome lay.

In some ways, he thought, with the abundance of fanged rock and the absence of vegetation and water, his surroundings were like the region of the Iron Peaks on Moros, where trainee legionaries went for individual survival tests. But at least in that place there would have been the moan of a mournful wind, and the crunch and slide of your boots over the rock, to prove that you were still alive. In this dreary place, airlessness meant an inhuman silence, bleak and disturbing, so that Keill felt like a disembodied ghost.

But he shook off the oppression that gathered in his mind, and began to make his way through the rocks – slowly and stealthily, controlling his movements now so that he kept low to the ground despite the low gravity, trying to step only on rock so that no tell-tale footprints would remain in the dust behind him.

At last, edging beneath an overhang that would have collapsed long before in normal gravity, he saw the dome.

It rose from the broad expanse of dust like a blister rises from human skin, but so bright in the reflected glare that it seemed to be made of mirrors. Around it, the dust was crisscrossed with the tracks of many boots, from the comings and goings of the dome's nine occupants. But at the moment there was no one in sight, no sign of movement or activity around the dome.

He drew back behind the screening rock and began a cautious circling, wanting to examine the dome from all sides, and most especially to locate its entrance.

Keill.

Glr's voice within his mind – and a tone of some urgency in the one word.

Your ship's sensors report another ship nearby. On a course for a landing.

As before, Keill concentrated, to form the reply in his mind. '*Will it overfly your position?*'

No, its course will bring it down near the dome, from the bright side. I will not be detected.

That was some luck, anyway, Keill thought to himself. But he wished that the other ship could have delayed its arrival awhile. Even so, he thought, if he could get close enough to the landing without being seen, and watch the men that disembarked, he might learn something.

He knew perfectly well, with a calm and untroubled sureness, that he would eventually have to try to enter the dome, no matter how many men were waiting inside. But he also had no intention of going in too blindly – not if he could manage a careful study of the opposition, or some of them, beforehand.

He wound his way as swiftly as he could through the rocks, still circling the dome but at no time exposing himself to it. Then he felt the ground tremble slightly beneath his feet. And at the same time Glr's voice reached into his mind again.

Sensors indicate the ship is landing. It seems to be the cruiser.

An image began to form in Keill's mind, projected by Glr – of the dome, squatting in its empty stretch of ground, and on the edge of that plain a ship coming in to land. The ship was recognizably a cruiser, but Glr's mind had added a few touches of her own – a great plume of fire from the ship's drive, and an evil face painted on to the front of the ship, all jagged teeth and cruel, slanted eyes.

'Thanks,' Keill said sardonically. '*Very artistic.*'

Better than a map, is it not? asked Glr, her laughter bubbling.

'*Much better. Be quiet now, while I go and look.*'

The heavy vibrations set up by the cruiser's landing increased steadily as he crept forward, until – crouching within the solid blackness of a tall rock's shadow – he was again at the edge of the plain.

The vibrations eased and stopped. The cruiser was down. Keill leaned forward to peer round the rock that sheltered him – and at once jerked his head back.

The cruiser had landed about three hundred metres away.

And beyond it, he had seen the entrance of the dome – its airlock open and spacesuited men emerging, moving at speed in the same long, leaping strides that Keill had used earlier.

He flattened himself against the rock. If any of those men, or the men in the ship, had glanced his way – and if his helmet had glinted even for an instant in the brilliant light . . .

It was an outside chance – but it was possible. Time to move.

But he did not retrace his steps. He drifted with slow caution from rock to rock towards where the cruiser had settled. Whatever the risk, he was not going to pass up a chance to see whatever might be seen.

Soon he had spotted another vantage point at the edge of the open area. When he reached it, he saw, he would be able to observe the ship and the dome while staying safely hidden in a bulge of deep shadow. He began to circle an outcropping, moving towards that point.

And he came face to face with two men, rounding the outcropping from the other direction.

Their faceplates, like Keill's, were darkened against the glare, revealing nothing. But one of them was wearing a spacesuit identical to Keill's – with the blue circlet of the Legions gleaming from helmet and chest.

And both men were holding weapons, ready in their hands.

Keill identified the guns at a glance, and with some distaste. Janglers, they were called – stubby pistols with ugly, flared, bell-shaped muzzles. They discharged a field that set up interference with the human nervous system – which caused, at the very least, indescribable pain. The guns were a sadist's weapon, outlawed on many worlds, and never, as Keill well knew, carried by legionaries.

He stood calmly where he was, making no motion towards his own weapon, while the other two took a tentative step towards him. The one in the Legion spacesuit lifted a gloved hand to his helmet, touching the switch that activated the man-to-man communicator.

'That you, Jiker?' The voice within Keill's helmet was metallic, distorted by the communicator.

Keill felt relieved. Of course there were two men on Creffa wearing full legionary uniform, which obviously included spacesuits. This one, seeing Keill's suit, naturally thought he was looking at his fellow impostor.

Keill flicked his own helmet switch. 'Yeah, it's me,' he said gruffly, knowing his voice would be just as distorted in the other man's ears.

But to his surprise the other raised his gun menacingly.

'The hell it is,' said the voice in Keill's helmet. '*I'm* Jiker.'

Keill's hand flashed, and his gun leaped from his belt. But the other man had only to press the firing stud on the jangler. And pure, raging agony reached out and grasped Keill's body like a monstrous fist.

Dimly he heard himself cry out, dimly he felt himself twisting, jerking, beginning to fall.

Then he heard and felt nothing at all.

chapter eleven

Keill awoke to the clamour of his own name being shouted, over and over.

No, not shouted, he realized. It was Glr's mental call, as penetrating as a cry of fear.

'*Stop it*,' he thought, raising one hand to his head, which was throbbing dully. '*I'm here*.'

Relief flooded into his mind from Glr's. *What happened? Where are you?*

Keill's probing fingers found a raised and tender bump on his head, and the slight roughness of dried blood. '*I must have bounced my head around in my helmet when I fell. As for where I am . . .*'

He looked around. He was lying on a hard bunk in a small, metal-walled cubicle – which he recognized as the usual cramped sleeping quarters for men in a space-dome. The air smelled stale and musty, but was breathable – and he was his normal weight, which meant that some form of artificial gravity was operating in the dome. His spacesuit had been stripped off him and flung untidily in one corner – though his energy gun, predictably, was not with it.

'*I'm inside the dome, and I'm in one piece*.' He swung up to a sitting position, ignoring the headache. One thing about the janglers, he thought to himself – for all the pain they caused, it stopped instantly when the weapon was deactivated. Though there could sometimes be serious after-effects . . .

What now? Glr asked.

'*You stay there, and stay quiet awhile. The door is probably guarded, and I'm going to . . .*'

Whatever it was, he was not able to do it. The door swung

open, and two men entered. Both were carrying guns, and they separated as they entered, moving to either side of Keill and keeping their weapons trained on him, all very professionally.

One of them, holding a jangler, was thin, wiry, with a long jaw and small, glittering eyes. The other was heavy-set and swarthy, with a nose that seemed to have been broken many times. And he had Keill's own beam-gun in his hand.

Both were wearing legionary uniforms.

'Y've come round, have y'?' the thin one said. 'Thought y' might've cracked y'r skull.' He grinned, a mouthful of small, yellow teeth. 'Nice trick, that, wasn't it? Askin' y' if y' was me? Ol' Rish here, he would've answered different, wouldn't y', Rish?'

The heavy-set man grunted, never taking his eyes from Keill. So the thin one was Jiker, the one who had shot Keill. And, yes, it had been a good trick. But Keill remained silent, studying the two men, judging their abilities, doubting if he would have much of a chance to move against two guns, but poised and ready if even the edge of a chance offered itself.

'Nothin' t' say t' y'r brother legionaries?' Jiker went on. His laugh was high-pitched and ugly.

'Where did you get the uniforms?' Keill asked, his voice as expressionless as his face.

'Took 'em off a ship that just came floatin' by,' Jiker grinned. 'Boys wearin' 'em didn't have use for 'em, not any more.'

'Where was that?' Keill asked.

'Just off good ol' Moros,' Jiker said, snickering. 'You remember Moros, don't y', boy?'

'Why were you there?' Much could be learned from talkative men, Keill knew, if they could be kept talking.

Jiker seemed all too ready to chatter. 'We like it there, don't we, Rish? Quietest place y' ever saw – real peaceful now. Like the boss said, when we did the last sweep . . .'

'Jiker!'

The voice from the doorway was deep, resonant, musical,

seeming effortlessly to fill the room. Jiker's thin mouth snapped shut, and he paled slightly beneath his spacer's sunburn as he glanced towards the door.

The bare-chested man who was entering the cubicle had to stoop, and to turn his vast shoulders sideways, to pass through the doorway. Here was the leader of the original three false legionaries – the half-naked giant who had gazed at Keill, and laughed, that frustrating day on the spaceport of Saltrenius.

He was smiling now, unpleasantly. 'Jiker, one of these days I think I will send you for a walk outside without a suit, and see if you can talk in vacuum.'

The threat seemed all the more vicious for having been made in that easy, melodious voice. Then the giant turned to inspect Keill – who countered with an inspection of his own.

The enormous, smoothly muscled bulk of the man was belied by the lightness of his step, the control of his movements. Here was no lumbering man-mountain, Keill saw, but a man who was as athletic and co-ordinated as he was powerful. Which made him all the more formidable.

Probably from one of the altered worlds, Keill surmised. The hairlessness, the bronze skin were indications. But there was something else . . .

He remembered the words of the newsman back on Saltrenius, which seemed so long ago. About the strange markings round the throat and belly of the giant. The marks were plainly visible to Keill – looking very much like raised, narrow ridges of scar tissue, evenly and completely encircling the powerful neck and abdomen. Then Keill looked again, and his skin crawled.

The ridges seemed to be *moving*. Writhing, swelling slightly. As if serpentine things with lives of their own were curled round the giant's body, just beneath the skin.

The giant's malicious smile widened as he surveyed Keill.

'So we have finally caught one, have we?' His chuckle resounded in the narrow room. 'And, I believe, the very one who was hurrying to make our acquaintance on Saltrenius. What took you so long to pay us a visit, legionary?'

Keill said nothing, watching the giant impassively.

'Taking refuge in silence, I see. Very well – we shall go through the formalities. Your name and rank?'

'Keill Randor, Group Leader of the fourth Strike Group of the 41st Legion.' Keill's voice was flat and cold.

'Of the planet Moros,' said the giant. 'Is that not how the ritual went on?'

Keill let the question pass. 'Gloating is a pastime of small minds. Do you have a name, gloater?'

The giant's smile faded for an instant, then returned. 'Ah, the legendary fighting spirit of the Legions is not quelled. Yes, Keill Randor, you may know my name – for the short while that you have left to know anything. I am the Lord Thr'un of Irruq-hoa.'

Keill raised a sardonic eyebrow. He had never heard of a planet called Irruq-hoa, but then there were many planets he had never heard of. He did know that aristocratic titles were common in many human societies through the galaxy. But it was an odd distinction for the leader of a gang like this to bear.

'Why is a lord of Irruq-hoa sitting on a moon of Saltrenius pretending to be a legionary?'

The giant's laughter boomed. 'On my world, we have a species of water creature that is hardly more than a large stomach, with filters. It sits quietly across the current of the stream, and other creatures swim blindly in, to be eaten. I have been waiting here to eat you, legionary.'

'On my planet,' Keill replied coldly, 'there was a poisonous reptile that had the ability to disguise itself as other, less vicious creatures. We always killed them, whenever we discovered one.'

'I am the reptile in disguise, am I?' laughed Thr'un. 'And you would like to kill me, I am sure.' He stepped forward, looming over Keill, the eerie markings jutting and squirming beneath his skin. 'It would be interesting to let you try, Randor. I have often wondered how the famous fighting skills of the Legions would measure up to those of the ... to mine.'

Keill had not missed the broken sentence. 'To those of the what?'

Thr'un smiled. 'So many questions. But it is I who have questions that are to be answered.' He moved back, folding his huge arms. 'First answer me this, Randor. How many other legionaries have survived?'

Keill nodded thoughtfully. 'So I am the first, as you said, to fall into your trap. I doubt if the others will be so careless.'

'What others?' the giant hissed. 'Where?'

Letting his eyes shift away from Thr'un, Keill assumed an expression of dismay, as if he had said more than he intended. 'Perhaps there are no others. I ... I don't know.'

'You will tell me!' Thr'un bellowed.

Keill bent his head and stared steadfastly at the floor, giving a perfect portrayal of a man determined not to give away a secret.

The giant snorted, and gestured at Jiker and Rish. 'Bring him along,' he ordered. 'You may tie him down and jangle him a little until he feels more conversational.'

Thr'un turned and went abruptly out, and Keill raised his head to confront the muzzles of the guns in the other men's hands, and the unholy gleam of pleasure in their eyes.

They guided him into a corridor that ran outside the cubicle, both men staying well behind him and staying on opposite sides of the corridor, so that even Keill could not hope to turn and lunge at both together. So he went without argument, using his chance to examine what he could see of the layout of the dome.

It seemed to follow the basic, standard shape of most space-domes. It was ovoid, and on two levels. The upper one would normally be a hemisphere of metal and plastic, topped with a broad lens-like circle of plastiglass and used primarily for observation, communication and the like. So Keill knew from the flat, blank ceiling that he must be on the lower level.

Most space-domes had one wide corridor running round the circumference of the lower level, just inside the tough outer hull. That main corridor would surround all the various functioning sections of the dome – like workrooms and laboratories, sleeping quarters, communal eating and recreation areas – along with the usual life-support systems, storage rooms and so on. And these would be connected by narrower passages that would each join up at some point with the main outer corridor.

So it seemed to be, in this case. The passage they had entered from the cubicle led to a broad, curving corridor as Keill had expected. A quick glance over his shoulder and he had exactly what he needed for his bearings – because he had glimpsed, behind them, the broad and heavy hatchway of an airlock. That had to be the dome's entrance – almost certainly its only one.

They moved along the main corridor, then soon turned down another of the narrow connecting passages. There the two armed men had to walk nearly shoulder to shoulder, but even so it would have been insanely risky for Keill to turn on them. Anyway, there was too much he still wanted to find out – and, he hoped, there might be better chances for escape later.

In a moment they came to a doorway opening off the passage, and the two urged Keill through it. It might once have been a laboratory, when the dome was serving its original purpose of scientific research. Now it was disused and empty, except for a low, heavy metal platform, which had once probably held an assortment of machinery and equipment.

Now, apparently, it was to hold Keill Randor.

'Get on there,' Jiker snarled, with a gesture of the jangler. 'On y'r back.'

Keill did as he was told, calmly, though he could guess what was to come. But Rish was holding the beam-gun aimed unerringly at Keill's head, and looked only too ready to use it.

Jiker stooped and took several metal bands and clamps from beneath the platform, obviously well prepared beforehand for their purpose. He fastened the bands tightly across Keill, clamping him to the bare metal surface so that he was immobilized – held by wrists and ankles, and by bands across chest and thighs.

'Now,' Jiker said, licking thin lips, 'think about them questions the boss asked y'.'

He raised the jangler and pressed the stud.

The agony flooded in. It was as if every nerve-end was being dragged forcibly from its place, to be dipped in acid and hacked at by a saw-toothed blade. Keill's body contorted, convulsed, threshing within the confines of the bands that held him – and blood streamed from his lip where he had sunk his teeth in to keep from screaming.

Then, instantly, the pain was gone. Breathing heavily, he licked his torn lip and glared with hatred at the grinning face of Jiker.

'Nice, was it? Anythin' t' say yet?'

Wordless, Keill looked away.

'Right, take as long as y' like. Plenty more where that came from.'

Jiker raised his gun again, glee in his eyes.

And again the murderous pain.

And again . . . And again . . .

After what may have been the sixth time, or the tenth – Keill could no longer be sure – he became aware that the giant had entered the room. For a time there was a pause while Thr'un consulted with his men, and Keill could assess his damage.

His body ached with bruising where the convulsions had thrust him against the metal bands. His lip was swollen and throbbing. And his head seemed to have become a size larger, so ferocious was the ache that filled it. But, tentatively moving his neck and as much of the rest of himself as he could, he knew that he still had command of his body, that he was not seriously injured.

Then the giant loomed over him.

'You seem determined to suffer,' said the melodious bass voice. 'As I would have expected. Are you any closer to telling me what I wish to know?'

Keill neither spoke nor looked at him.

'Also as I would have expected,' Thr'un said with an exaggerated sigh. 'The Legions made their men little more than robots, blindly following the demands of their masters.'

An odd emphasis in the words gave Keill the glimmer of an idea. Finding what was left of his voice, he croaked, 'Do you not follow *your* masters?'

Thr'un took the bait. 'My Master,' he began, 'does not require me . . .'

He stopped abruptly, glowering down at Keill. 'Very crafty, legionary.' The voice rumbled deep and deadly. 'You have been trying hard, have you not, to learn what you can. But you have learned nothing. And even if I were able to reveal to you the name and whereabouts of the Master, you would not live long enough to make use of that knowledge.'

Keill ignored the death threat, his mind grasping and examining the rest of the speech. A 'Master'? Who set up this trap on Creffa, and also sent the men on sweeps near Moros, as Jiker had said? Who seemed to give his minions something of a free hand? And whose name and whereabouts Thr'un was not 'able' to reveal?

It was all beginning to sound like something he had heard before.

He tried to focus his mind, to contact Glr and pass on what he had learned. Perhaps the little alien could make more sense out of these vague hints. Or perhaps the Overseers . . .

But then the giant was speaking again, distracting him. 'You may now decide, Randor. Tell me of these other survivors, and you have a chance to keep your useless life. Stay silent, and you will die, now, in a most unpleasant manner.'

Keill smiled coldly. 'As far as I know, there are no others. I have met none, I have heard of none.'

'Lies!' boomed the giant, and gestured to Jiker. The thin man hurried forward, grinning.

While Rish kept his beam-gun steadily on Keill, Jiker removed two of the bonds – those across his body – leaving him clamped only by his wrists and ankles.

'As you know,' Thr'un said malevolently, 'janglers do not themselves kill. But you will also know that the convulsions they cause can be very severe. A man who might happen to be held by hands and feet might suffer a great deal of damage. He is likely to bend himself almost in two – and his neck or his spine will snap as if they were glass.'

Keill said nothing, still striving to gather his concentration, to reach Glr.

'Have you an answer now to my question?' Thr'un bellowed.

But Keill ignored him, for the voice of Glr had slid into his mind.

Keill, if you are projecting, I cannot fix on it. It is too muzzy. Try harder – because there is trouble. I sense two humans moving nearby, probably searching for the ship.

As expected, Keill thought, the giant had sent men out to look for their captive's ship. With a supreme effort, he gathered his thought. *'Glr, take off at once, and stay in space on the dark side. If you hear nothing more from me, tell the Overseers that I . . .'*

But he was unable to continue the message, for Thr'un was bellowing again, drawing his attention.

'As you wish, legionary! If there are others, some will no doubt visit me soon. They may prove more co-operative. I have no more use for you!' He turned to Jiker. 'Go ahead.'

Jiker began his high-pitched titter as he took aim. Then the jangler flared.

As before, Keill's body twisted, writhed, flexed – and now

arched high off the metal surface. Arched in an impossible curve, jerking and threshing, only his arms and his feet held still.

Then there was a sickening, grinding crack.

Jiker released the firing stud, and Keill's body slumped down, limp and motionless.

chapter twelve

The intense, crushing pain that continued within his body proved, to Keill's half-conscious surprise, that he was still alive. It also told him that he would probably not live for much longer.

The pain clawed at every segment of his body. Each muscle and joint was in torment, but most of all his neck and lower back. He had clearly broken his spine, as Thr'un had indicated. Perhaps his spinal cord still held, temporarily, but he would not have long before it too gave way. He would probably be dead even before Thr'un or his men got round to finishing him off.

He felt no fear, no self-pity – just an edge of regret that he had achieved so little against Thr'un and his false legionaries. But at least he had gathered a few hints, which he still had to pass on to Glr. He fought with the haze in his mind, fought to focus his thoughts, to make contact again with the alien. But the pain, and voices dimly heard, intruded. One of the voices was Thr'un's, from some distance away – as if the giant had turned to leave, after Keill's collapse, and was issuing orders from the doorway.

'. . . won't have survived that,' the deep bass voice was saying. 'Strip off the uniform for one of the other men to use.'

'Whatd' we do with th' body?' Jiker's thin voice.

'Put it in the airlock, and some of the others can take it to the ship. We'll throw it out when we next visit the planet, and let it burn in atmosphere.'

Jiker began to say something else, but Keill didn't hear – for Glr was in his mind, fear and worry plain in the inner voice.

Keill clutched at his concentration, and in pain-filled bursts of thought, told Glr what had happened.

In the midst of the anxiety pouring from Glr's mind, he heard – astonishingly – the rise of the alien's silent laughter.

Keill, you are a hardhead! Glr cried. *Clinging to your doubts still – even to convince yourself that you're dying!*

Clearly, Keill thought, he had not managed to project properly, and Glr had misunderstood. He began to try again, but the alien interrupted.

No, I received you properly. Don't you see? Talis told you the simple truth. Nothing those men could do could break so much as your little finger!

The hope that ballooned up within Keill was instantly crushed by disbelief. The agony in his back was very real . . .

Of course it is! Glr replied. *The weapon put every muscle and tendon under terrible stress – that is what hurts! But nothing is broken! Nothing can be!*

Hope seeped back, determined. The pain from aching ligaments? The terrible cracking sound merely from joints shifting under the strain, as a man can crack his knuckles without damage?

He tried tentatively to move his body, half-expecting that he might be paralysed. But it moved – torso shifting, knees rising. As he moved, the pain flared, then eased, slightly. And hope burst forth undiminished.

It seemed to be true! He was probably suffering only from a ferocious stretching and twisting. And a lifetime of gruelling Legion exercises, which were focused on stretching and twisting, had made his body supple beyond most people's imaginings. He had very likely pulled a muscle or two, strained ligaments – but he was intact, he was functional. It might hurt, but his body would do his bidding.

By then it was time for it to do so. The whole exchange with Glr, at the incalculable speed of thought, had taken place while Jiker and Rish were turning back towards him from the door. The giant Thr'un had presumably left the room. And his two men, only glancing at Keill who was again lying as limp as he could, began at once to release the clamps that held him to the metal platform.

Then Jiker's sharp eyes registered the faint movement of Keill's chest, with his breathing.

'Sunfires,' Jiker gasped, 'he's still alive!'

Keill remained motionless, and made his breath rasp in his throat.

'Not f'r long, I reckon,' Rish grunted. 'Give him another burst.'

Keill sent out a sharp mental call. '*Glr, come in now, quickly, and overfly the dome, as low as you can.*'

I hear and obey, came the laughing reply.

Jiker was taking a tentative step forward. 'Can't be faking – not after what we gave him. Must be a lot stronger 'n he looks.'

Keill made his chest heave, gave a choking rattle in his throat, then sagged, not breathing.

Jiker took another stride forward, and bent over him, listening.

And with the howling, throbbing roar of a thousand devils, Keill's spaceship thundered past overhead, no more than a man's height from the upper surface of the dome.

Both men jerked their heads up, gaping fearfully.

And Keill reached, grasped Jiker's tunic, shifted his hips for leverage, and flung the skinny man into Rish's face.

Every muscle of his back shrieked its displeasure, but it was an entirely bearable pain. He swung round and came to his feet, just as Rish, face contorted with anger, also scrambled up-right. Both men had dropped their guns as they sprawled, but Rish was too enraged to think about weapons. He lowered his head like a bull, and charged.

Keill swayed aside, grasped and jerked at a meaty shoulder so that the charge became a headlong plunge.

The impact of Rish's forehead on the corner of the metal platform echoed dully in the room. The heavy man sagged to the floor, his face a mask of blood, an indentation showing where a segment of his skull had been crushed back into his brain.

Keill did not glance at the corpse, for Jiker was scrabbling across the floor towards one of the guns. Keill sprang to intercept him – grasping him by the belt and hurling him across the room, where he bounced from the wall and lay huddled. Then Keill scooped up both the jangler and his own energy-gun.

'Now it's your turn to do a little dance,' he growled.

Jiker was jibbering with fear. 'How . . . how c'n you be alive?'

'Worry about your own life,' Keill said. 'The other men – where will they be?'

'Dunno,' Jiker gabbled. 'Canteen, maybe – no!' His voice rose thinly as Keill aimed the jangler at him. 'They'll be suitin' up – to go out an' see what that was just went by!'

Keill flung out a mental message. '*Glr, circle back and disable their ship. Then bring the ship down and fire a blast or two just in front of the dome's entrance.*'

To keep them penned up inside? Glr said, doubtfully.

'*Yes.*' There was a cold deadliness in the mental tone. '*I want them all in here, with me.*'

As you wish, said Glr.

Keill had not taken his eyes from Jiker. 'Where will the men be, suiting up?'

'Equipment room, down th' other end by th' entrance.'

'And Thr'un?'

'Maybe with 'em . . . Maybe up in th' dome, where he stays most 'f th' time . . .' An evil glint lit up Jiker's eyes. 'Y' won't get past him, y'know! He'll take y' apart! He ain't human!'

Keill was about to demand more detail on that interesting point when the door to the chamber was flung open.

One of the other men burst in, obviously sent to collect Jiker and Rish. The pass Glr had made in the ship had produced action. Thr'un would be organizing his men to face a possible attack.

But Keill spun and fired – with the beam-gun – before the

newcomer could open his mouth. The man screamed and toppled, a small flame licking for an instant at the edge of the hole burned by the energy gun in the centre of his chest. And in that instant Jiker scrambled to his feet and lunged desperately at Keill.

Effortlessly Keill stepped within the reach of the frantically clawing fingers and drove a short, jabbing punch at the side of the long jaw. Anger and left-over pain put extra venom behind his fist – and the angle of Jiker's head, as his body sprawled, showed that it was not only janglers that broke necks.

Beneath his feet the floor quivered, heavy vibrations shaking the rock foundation of the dome. That would be Glr, making short work of the cruiser.

Keill moved quickly towards the door, bending over the man he had shot, freeing his gun. A needler, just for variety. But not much more useful to Keill than the jangler. He dropped both weapons on the floor, and smashed them with two driving blows of his heel. His own beam-gun would be all the weapon he would need.

There had been eight men, and Thr'un had made nine. Now there were five, besides the giant.

More vibrations underfoot – and then the voice of Glr in Keill's mind.

At the entrance, as requested. Two men in spacesuits had started to come out. They have gone back in at some speed.

'Good,' Keill replied. *'Stay there and keep watch. And don't speak for a while – I'm going to be busy.'*

Gun in hand, he sprang through the door and moved away along the narrow passage.

There had been no one in the passage – and as Keill came to its junction with the wide outer corridor, and peered carefully round the corner, there was still no one in sight. No doubt most of the remaining men were collected at the other end of the dome, near the airlocks, as Jiker had said. All their attention would be on the spaceship – with its Legion markings –

guarding the dome's entrance. The last thing they would expect would be one man attacking them from within.

And, because that one man was an armed legionary of Moros, in full fighting readiness and with a good many scores to settle, it was all too likely that it would be the *last* thing they would expect.

Keill turned into the corridor and moved swiftly and silently along it, hugging the inner wall. His movements seemed to have eased the pain from his strained and tortured muscles, and he moved as lightly and fluidly as he ever did. He slowed his pace as he neared the opening of another connecting passage. A careful glance round – and again no one. But soon, he was certain, the curving main corridor would reveal the opening of the airlock at the dome's entrance . . .

And there it was; and two men in space suits, with guns in their hands – energy guns. They hesitated only for a second, astonished at the sight of him, then jerked up their guns and fired.

Keill dived full length straight ahead. His left hand slapped on the smooth metal floor to break his fall, as the beams from the others' guns sizzled above his head. Then he was sliding a few paces, full length on the floor, but his own gun was rock-steady in his right hand, blazing out its deadliness.

The two men dropped with a clatter, and Keill was up again. To the left of the spacesuited bodies, a doorway that had to be the end chamber where the others were gathered. Three left now, besides the giant.

He flattened against the wall, swiftly glanced round the edge of the door and drew back. Energy beams hissed past, biting into the doorframe, the metal sliding and dripping as it melted. Two of them, waiting, hidden behind metal cases in what must be the equipment room. He could hear their voices, high-pitched and nervous in the face of this unexpected attack.

Beyond them, he had seen in that lightning glance, had been another doorway. And somewhere there was a third man . . .

He moved quietly away from the door. The two inside the

equipment room would keep for a moment – they were not likely to move. But the third man was probably trying to circle, to get behind Keill. Would he use the nearest connecting passage, the one Keill had just come past?

Apparently he would. Keill waited at the corner of the passage, ears straining, and caught the muffled slide of boots on metal as the man crept forward. Listening carefully, Keill waited – not a muscle moving, hardly breathing, as if he were carved in stone.

Another soft shuffle of a foot – nearer now. Carefully Keill weighed the distance and the timing, poising himself, silently shifting his gun to his left hand . . .

Then the other man put his head round the corner, and met the axe-edge of Keill's hand across his throat.

Keill caught the body as it collapsed, easing it soundlessly to the floor, ignoring the purple-black of the face as the man died swiftly from a crushed larynx. Silent as before, he drifted along the narrow connecting passage, rounded the corner, then let his boots ring solidly on the metal as he stepped through the doorway into the chamber behind the last two men who waited, watching nervously in the wrong direction.

They swung round in panic, wildly trying to bring their guns to bear, and Keill dropped them with one shot apiece.

And now there was only Thr'un.

A quick but careful survey of the remainder of the dome's lower level confirmed what Jiker had said. The giant was certainly on the upper level – where he had no doubt gone to look out at the Legion ship that lay in wait at the dome's entrance.

Keill paused at the bottom of the stairs that led to the upper level, staring up at the curving wall, with a patch of stars glinting through the plastiglass at the crest of the dome. One set of stairs, which emerged through the floor of the top level, so that at the top Keill would be in full view of the waiting Thr'un.

He ghosted up a few steps in total silence, then halted,

crouching, and projected a call. '*Glr – another diversion. Fire a blast over the dome, as close as you can.*'

At your service, came the cheerful reply.

The plastiglass flared with eerie light as the narrow beam of energy blazed past overhead. In the same instant Keill sprang up the remaining stairs, dived and rolled.

Another, narrower beam flashed centimetres away from where he had been, burning deep into the floor. But Keill had found refuge behind a heap of discarded cases, and lay there, listening carefully, looking over his surroundings.

Clearly Thr'un's men had seen no need to be tidy-minded in their occupancy of the dome. Nor had the scientific group who had first used the structure been any more inclined to neatness when they left. The upper level, which was one large chamber with the dome itself as ceiling, was filled with clutter and rubble.

There were discarded cases and containers of every size and shape, scattered and heaped at random. There were what seemed to be stacks of spare parts for machinery, and segments of scientific equipment, probably damaged and thrown aside as irreparable. There were even a few mounds of rock – no doubt samples from the surface of the moon, left behind after examination.

It all meant useful cover, for anyone wishing to keep hidden in the wide chamber. But it was cover for Thr'un as much as Keill.

Then Keill saw that there was a considerable cleared space along one side of the chamber – a space that was dominated by a tall bank of equipment, apparently in working order.

Communications equipment, without doubt. Perhaps for Thr'un to maintain contact with his 'Master'?

A faint rustle to Keill's left. The giant was circling, stalking, seeking a chance for another shot with his beam-gun.

Keep moving, Keill told himself, edging soundlessly away to his right. It was his only direction – yet he regretted it, for

114

he was being driven away from the stairs, being cut off from the only way out. No matter, he thought. If he'd been sensible, he would never have climbed the stairs – but merely have gone out to his ship and blasted the dome to cinders. But somehow he had wanted to face the giant this way. And there was always the chance that more useful information might be forthcoming.

The energy beam hissed past him, and a metal canister on a heap of rubbish fell away, a gaping hole melted into its surface. Keill ducked, moving swiftly – and as he did so, the rich bass voice of Thr'un echoed musically through the chamber.

'Welcome, legionary. You seem amazingly difficult to kill – but I promise you, you will not leave here alive.'

chapter thirteen

Keill did not reply, but took advantage of the sound of the resonant voice to move more swiftly. Only a few strides now, and he would be behind the heavy bank of equipment that was some complex form of communicator. There was a chance that Thr'un would not wish to burn through that, to reach him.

'As close-mouthed as ever, Randor?' called the giant. He, too, had moved, as the direction of his voice showed. 'I would have thought you would have a few last words.'

Again, covered by the rolling echoes of Thr'un's voice, Keill moved. For an instant he was fully exposed in the cleared area, but his speed saved him. He felt the blistering heat of the energy beam just above his head as he dived and rolled, coming to rest behind the communicator cabinet. Its metal bulk rose comfortingly above him, nearly his own height.

'You are mistaken,' Thr'un said, 'if you think that will protect you.' To underline the words, the energy beam bit at the corner of the communicator. Molten metal hissed and dripped.

'And you are mistaken,' Keill shouted, 'if you think killing me will save you. My . . . companion in the ship still has you trapped.'

'Yes, that was clever of you,' Thr'un mocked. His voice indicated that he was moving slowly closer. 'I had not imagined that there was someone in your ship – you were alone, were you not, on Saltrenius? Who is it out there, another legionary?'

'As full of questions as ever, Thr'un?' Keill said, mimicking the giant's earlier words. 'Still intending to report dutifully to your Master?'

Keill was aware that the giant wanted to keep him talking, to put him off-guard when the final attack came. But the trick might work in reverse. Certainly Thr'un seemed to enjoy the sound of his own voice . . .

'I do not report to the Master,' Thr'un sneered. 'Only the One reports.'

Keill sat up at that. More intriguing hints and mysteries. Could he jolt more information out of the giant – providing he had time to do so?

'And the "One" would be the head of your group that you nearly told me about?'

'Clever again,' Thr'un growled. He was even closer now. His energy gun crackled again, and a corner of the communicator sagged, something within it bursting briefly into flame. Keill paid scant attention.

'Is he as insane as you, or your cowardly Master?' he called.

'You prattle of things beyond your knowledge!' Th'run replied, voice rumbling deep with anger.

'Knowledge?' Keill said. He sensed that the moment of attack was near, and spoke quickly, hardly thinking about what he was saying. 'I know what you are, and who you serve. I know your Master is the destroyer of my world and my people. And I know that he has a madman's dream of wrecking the galaxy with warfare, and ruling over its ruins!'

Surprise joined the anger in Thr'un's voice. 'You know more than you should, legionary. More than I imagined. The Master will be interested.'

Again his beam-gun blazed, and there was a flash and a muffled explosion deep in the bowels of the bank of equipment. Keill drew back slightly as the metal that sheltered him grew hot to the touch. But he moved by reflex, hardly aware – for his mind was dazedly trying to assimilate what had just been said.

He had hurled his wild accusations, based on the story old Talis had told, in order to provoke Thr'un into revealing the true nature of the 'Master' who directed him. He had not imagined for a moment . . .

But it had happened. Thr'un had *confirmed* the fantastic things Keill had said.

Which meant that the Overseers' story about the Warlord . . . was true.

As true as Talis's statement about the bones of Keill's body.

He shook his head, trying to clear it, to re-orient himself. Think about it later, he told himself savagely, or you won't live to think at all.

Thr'un's voice had last come from a point that must be on, or near, the edge of the cleared area. Silently Keill eased his way to the right, crouching at the corner of the communicator, concentrating, focusing energy and power into his legs. Make him speak again, he thought. Pinpoint his position.

'Your Master won't be pleased at what has happened here, Thr'un,' he called. 'A failure is executed – isn't that the way of the Warlord?'

'Warlord, you call him?' Thr'un rumbled. 'An apt name. Yes, he has his way with failure. But I have not failed, legionary. I was sent here to complete the task I began – to clear the galaxy of your Legions. And I will complete it!'

The implication of the words struck Keill at once, and the hatred and rage that rose in him seemed to fill his veins with fire. '*You*? You are the destroyer?'

'It was I,' the giant gloated, 'who sent the radiation capsules into the atmosphere of Moros. A laughably simple task. Miniature capsules, made by the genius of the Master, hidden in an innocent shipment of grain. Your Legions suspected nothing. And then, on the signal, the chain reaction . . .'

But Keill did not let him finish. Fury reinforced his strength as he exploded into a surging leap – not sideways round the corner of the communicator, but straight up, in a mighty standing jump.

He was firing as he leaped, firing as his feet struck the top of

the melting, blackened machine, firing still as he sprang without pause out across the cleared area, at the throat of his enemy.

The giant had flung himself to one side to dodge the deluge
of energy blasts, and that movement and Keill's speed threw
his own aim off. Energy beams sizzled past Keill as he charged
– and then scalding pain bit deep into his right shoulder as one
of the erratic beams found him, spinning him off-balance,
hurling him to the floor.

His gun fell and slid out of reach – and then the giant,
moving with his own astonishing speed, was towering over
him, gun levelled at Keill's face.

Keill waited for the death shot, but Thr'un did nothing,
except let a cruel smile of satisfaction grow across his face.

'You see?' he said. 'I have not failed, after all.'

Keill looked at him with contempt. 'You won't have long
to gloat. My companion will know the moment I am dead –
and will destroy the dome with you in it.'

'Indeed? I doubt if he will know so quickly. No, I will have
no trouble in burning my way out of the rear of the dome and
dealing with your companion – after I have dealt with you.'

He widened his mocking smile, then glanced down at
Keill's shoulder, where blood seeped steadily through the
seared flesh.

'You are injured, which is a shame,' Thr'un said. 'Yet you
have proved a dangerous and resourceful opponent, and so
you can still be deemed worthy.'

To Keill's astonishment, Thr'un stepped back, and tossed
his beam-gun aside. 'Come, Randor, let me show you what I
know to be true – that the much-admired skill of the Legions
is nothing to the power of the Deathwing!'

Keill rose slowly to his feet, hardly able to believe what was
happening. 'Deathwing?'

Thr'un laughed expansively. 'You have not heard the name?
It is the Master's select force – his chosen lieutenants, who
serve his will throughout the galaxy. Men like myself, Randor,
from the altered worlds. Men to whom the Master has given

skills, and strengths, and power, beyond anything dreamed of by a puny legionary!' He raised his arms at his sides, muscles rolling under the naked bronze skin. 'See, Randor! See how your death will come!'

Keill's eyes widened with amazement and horror. The weird, ridged markings on the giant's body were moving again. Writhing, swelling – *opening* . . .

From beneath the skin, where the ridges encircled Thr'un's body, erupted *growths*. Swiftly they extended, upwards and downwards, flaring, fanning out. They were like slabs of thick and heavy leather, solid linked plates of a dark, unpleasantly muddy colour. And they protected the giant like armour.

From the band around the neck they spread out to cover the throat and the base of the skull, reaching down over the upper chest and back. Below, the abdominal armour extended to cover the loins, the belly and the kidneys, stretching up over the solar plexus and the lower ribs.

All the weaker points on the human body – from neck to thigh – were, on Thr'un, protected from harm.

Keill had backed away a step, involuntarily. But he saw the sadistic light in the giant's eyes, and fought to bring his shock and revulsion under control – willing his aching, wounded body into the poised relaxation of combat readiness. His right shoulder felt as if naked flame was still eating at his flesh. But it was not a crippling wound, he knew. Beyond the pain, he still had the use of the arm.

Yet he let it dangle limply, as if the shoulder was shattered. Over-confidence might be the only weakness that Thr'un would show.

Then the giant attacked, without warning.

Keill was nearly trapped by the speed and power of the rush. But he managed to dodge one blow, block another, and spin away out of reach. Instantly Thr'un was upon him again – and again Keill evaded the attack, twisting away.

It became the pattern of the fight. Keill remained on the defensive – dodging, blocking, circling, relying on his balance and speed of reflexes to preserve him. But it was a dangerous game. With his injury and loss of blood, and the after-effects of the jangler, he was likely to tire and weaken before Thr'un did. And he was still persisting in using only his left arm to defend himself.

Also, Thr'un was swift, immensely strong, and considerably skilled. Not, for all his boasting, up to Legion standards, Keill had soon realized. Thr'un's combat skills were a little too orthodox, a little too predictable and unimaginative.

But that offered small advantage – when the uncanny body armour protected him so well.

And Keill soon found out how well. Knowing that he could not last in a prolonged battle, he took the fight to Thr'un more and more, counter-attacking out of defence. But he found that striking the armour was like hitting a padded wall. The thick, leathery substance seemed to give slightly under any blow, absorbing its power, so that Thr'un was hardly troubled. Keill had to look for targets on the head or legs – and the giant, knowing he could leave his torso virtually undefended, could more easily block or evade, preventing Keill from landing an effective blow.

So they fought on, Keill still circling, defending, probing for an opening that seemed never to come – the giant still aggressive, confident. Each attack was a flurry of blows and counters, a blur of weaving, swaying bodies. The giant feinting with a straight right-hand slash at the belly, the left hand whipping across to chop at the neck – Keill sliding inside the blow, heel of the left hand driving up – Thr'un blocking and striking for the face in the same fluid motion – Keill dropping almost to one knee, a foot lashing out at a kneecap – Thr'un swivelling away from the kick, his own foot countering to smash at Keill's jaw – Keill rolling away, coming to his feet, fingers flickering out in a stab at the eyes as the giant leaped again, huge hands clutching . . .

Weariness began to seep into Keill's limbs, and his breathing grew heavier. His time was running out. Now the giant was reaching him more often, as Keill's energy flagged. Time and again only desperate reflex turned a crushing elbow-smash from Thr'un into a glancing graze, only reflex dragged his thigh around to deflect a hurtling kick to the groin. And each of these times Keill staggered, and a little more strength drained from his weary, damaged body.

But his mind was still a legionary's mind – controlled, disciplined, aware. He did not miss the glitter of anticipation and triumph in Thr'un's eyes whenever Keill staggered, or when one of Keill's attacks failed. And Keill did not hesitate when his mind weighed up the danger, and produced what could be his only, desperately risky chance to survive.

The giant was given to gloating, to over-confidence. He had already been led to believe that Keill had only one usable arm. Lead him on a little further . . .

Now as he circled and countered, Keill let his body sag even more, let himself stumble and catch himself more often, let his breathing become ragged panting.

The gleam grew in Thr'un's eyes, his teeth flashed in a victory smile, as he plunged in pursuit of his apparently collapsing opponent.

Any moment now, Keill told himself as he weakly swayed aside from a flailing boot, pretending to half-stagger before recovering. He circled again, moving carefully. The timing had to be perfect, Thr'un had to approach at exactly the right angle, and had to respond in exactly the right, orthodox, predictable way . . .

The giant hurtled forward, just as Keill wanted him to. And Keill swung his left fist, slowing the punch slightly, invitingly.

Thr'un took the invitation. One hand flashed up and grasped Keill's wrist, the other huge arm clamped his elbow. Then the giant pivoted, twisted, and threw.

In the microsecond before his feet left the floor, a flurry of images passed through Keill's mind. The unbelievable words of Talis, on the Overseers' asteroid – the aftermath of the torture session at the hands of Jiker and Rish – the reassuring words of Glr...

He had manoeuvred Thr'un into using a standard hold-and-throw, so basic in unarmed combat as to be almost instinctive. If performed properly, as Keill's body was swung up and across his arm should break neatly in about three places.

He had been sure that Thr'un, with the orthodoxy of his technique, would use the hold. And he had been sure that the giant would not miss a chance to cripple his opponent's other arm, after which he would no doubt take his time at kicking Keill to death.

But the arm . . . did not break.

Keill flexed his body as he arched through the air, and his feet thudded firmly on to the floor, instantly finding balance and leverage. The tendons in his left elbow shrieked with the wrenching pain, but held.

Thr'un, expecting a shattered arm within his grasp, but finding instead that he was holding an arm like a steel bar, was dragged forward for a fleeting instant, off-balance, exposed.

And Keill, oblivious to the blaze of agony in his injured shoulder, swung his right fist across in a short arc with precise timing, swivelling his perfectly poised body as he struck, so that all his weight, all his fury, all his vengeful hatred followed into and through the blow.

In the Martial Games of Moros, such a blow from the fist of Keill Randor had smashed through slabs of plasticrete piled nearly a metre high – had splintered a wooden post as thick as Keill's own waist – had once even crumpled and cracked a plate of niconium steel.

Now that fist struck lethally at Thr'un's temple, just above the ear where the skull is thinnest, and crushed it like paper.

The huge armoured body was flung away like a dry leaf in a storm, crashing to the floor with a heavy, echoing finality.

part four
Aftermath and beginning

chapter fourteen

The viewscreens showed the peaceful, star-glittering vastness of deep space. Far behind, on a tiny moon called Creffa, lay the molten, crumbled ruins of what had once been a gleaming space-dome, flattened by the guns of Keill's spaceship – the last thing Keill had done before his battle fury was spent, before he had sagged back to let Glr take the controls.

The little alien had taken the ship leaping out beyond the planetary system of Saltrenius, far into the welcoming reaches of space. There her strange, small hands had dressed Keill's shoulder, rubbed medication on his aching, tormented muscles and generally attended to all his hurts. Now Keill lay back, luxuriating in the restful clasp of the slingseat, and – with the ship under computer guidance – waited while Glr finished her long-range telepathic report to the Overseers.

At last the round eyes opened. *Talis regrets that the communicator on the dome had to be destroyed. It might have provided some directional fix.*

Keill shook his head. 'There wasn't much left of it before I destroyed the dome,' he said aloud.

Certainly the Overseers approve the dome's destruction, Glr said. *They wished no hints of what happened there left to be found by searchers from the Warlord.*

'Secrecy at all costs,' Keill intoned, hearing Glr's soft laughter in his mind.

Talis is very interested in your mention of the group called the Deathwing. He regrets you were not able to learn more about it.

'I beg his pardon,' Keill said sourly. 'That conversation ended a little abruptly.'

The mental laughter rose. *He understands that the Deathwing is a special force from which the Warlord selects his emissaries. But he wonders if you have any theories about the others in the group – especially the person whom Thr'un called 'the One'.*

'Not really. Except that if he's the leader of that group, and someone like Thr'un only a follower, he must be fairly impressive.'

Just so. Glr's imitation of Talis's favourite phrase made Keill grin. *The Overseers also ask if you have any doubts remaining, about what Talis told you during your stay with them.*

Doubts? Keill felt again the chill that had swept over him in that desperate moment of realization when, facing Thr'un, he had learned that the whole fearful story of the Warlord was true beyond all doubt.

'Only one,' he said grimly. 'That if I meet any more members of this Deathwing, I doubt if I'll survive the encounter.'

Glr's bright eyes shone with amusement as she relayed the message. *Talis is sure you will, now that you know more about what to expect. He is very pleased at being right about his assessment of your survival potential.*

'Fine,' Keill muttered. 'Tell him we're all very pleased here, too.'

He also hopes you will now confirm, Glr went on, *that you will act as the Overseers' emissary. To go on their behalf to worlds that are*

126

threatened by the Warlord – and to do what you can to oppose the threat.

Keill knew what his answer was, yet he hesitated. On *their* behalf? But he was still a legionary, if alone – and he had a job to do, an unspoken promise to keep, to the dead of Moros. He did not delude himself that the defeat of Thr'un was anything but a first, small step in keeping that promise. Somewhere the real enemy, the real destroyer, still lived, still strove to spread his deadly infection of violence and murder.

'Tell Talis,' he said slowly, 'that it is as much my fight as his – or more. Tell him that I will work with the Overseers, but not *for* them. I will accept advice and assistance, but not orders. Tell him that wherever I go, I will do what I can and what I must – but *my* way, without interference.'

Talis understands the conditions, and agrees.

'And do you come along as well?'

Of course, Glr laughed. *You would certainly never survive without me.*

Keill lay back in the slingseat. In his mind's eye an image formed – an image that always lurked on the edge of his imagination, that would probably always continue to lurk there. The image of the planet Moros as he last saw it – bathed in a glowing haze of lethal radiation, in which everything and everyone that Keill had loved had met their deaths.

And beyond that image, another, newer one. Like a black shadow across his inner vision. The dark mystery of the Warlord – and the shadow of the Deathwing.

The Overseers are waiting for your confirmation, Glr broke in.

'Tell the Overseers,' Keill said, 'confirmed. Absolutely confirmed.'